THE LONGING PATTERN

A FORBIDDEN LUST

HEATHER STOLTZ

plicit Press
Erotica Fiction

CHAPTER 1

DRUNK ON YOU

SONYA RAYNER'S *best friend takes her out for a final bash before her big internship at the Barrows Agency, one of the most prestigious boutique agencies in Los Angeles. She just wants to show Sonya a good time, but one shot turns to two, and before long, Sonya's party girl tendencies are out in full force. When she catches the eye of a handsome stranger, she lets herself be drawn into his web. They have a heated encounter but is there more to this handsome stranger than Sonya knows?*

Sonya Rayner eyed the shot glass like the blue liquid was really an alien's clever disguise and any moment it would burst to life and attack her face. She didn't quite catch what her friend, Beth, had said when she ordered the drink, and she had absolutely no idea of the content. Literally, *anything* could be in there, and usually, Sonya was on board with that. But she wasn't exactly feeling adventurous —not on the night before her first day at one of the biggest agencies in Hollywood. She couldn't roll through their hallowed doors with a hangover the size of Texas.

"Stop being such a wuss and drink it already," Beth said. "It's not going to kill you."

"And I should trust you why? Sorry, dear, I love you but you are not at all trustworthy."

"When have I ever led you astray?"

"More times than I can count. And I have a *job* now. I can't just drink like...I'm in college."

"You are in college."

"No. Tomorrow is the beginning of my summer internship, which means for three months I have to act like an adult."

Beth snorted. "It means for three months you get to act like a slave, busting your ass for the man and not even getting paid for it."

"I am getting paid for it."

"In cash?"

"No, in experience."

Beth shook her head. "Then it doesn't count as getting paid."

Sonya rolled her eyes. This wasn't the first time they had this debate, and she was pretty tired of it. The fact remained that this was an excellent opportunity for her and she fully intended to make the most of it. Plus, Dominic Barrows, the head of the agency, represented some major stars. Some of America's biggest names came strolling through their doors, and for one glorious summer, Sonya had full access and front row seats to the show. Not to mention, she'd probably get actual VIP passes for shows throughout the summer simply because her boss was their main guy.

As far as she could tell, there was no downside.

"Drink your fucking drink," Beth said, nudging her hand. "Come on girl. We're here to have fun one more night of fun before you become all boring and professional."

"So if I drink this, you won't drag me out drinking tomorrow night?"

"*Drag* you? Like I had to twist your arm. You're the one who wanted a drink, so drink the fuck up!"

Beth was right, Sonya had mentioned drinks first. Specifically, she had clutched her head and said she'd *kill for a drink,* citing her short nerves as the reason. Kill for *one* drink. So she could have the shot Beth bought for her—whatever the hell it was—and then stick to mineral water for the rest of the night, which would effectively kill the chances of a hangover. She'd be able to have her cake and eat it too—or have her shot and drink it too, as the case may be.

"Okay. Just this one, though. I'm serious, Beth, I don't want to get drunk tonight."

"Nobody's got a gun to your head."

"Bottoms up."

"Wait." Beth lifted her shot glass. "To a happy and successful internship. I know this means a lot to you. You're going to knock them dead."

Sonya's eyes suddenly felt prickly, and she downed the drink before she could get all emotional. She didn't often get to see her roommate's soft and squishy side, but it was her favorite part of her friend. She was one of the very few who ever got to see it.

"And may you have a great summer full of sex, drugs, and rock and roll."

"Woo! Now you're speaking my language!"

They touched their glasses together and then flung their heads back, flooding their systems with the overwhelming booze. She definitely tasted tequila—not to mention the kickback that always got her right in the chest—but there was something fruity in there and something that tasted like cinnamon.

"Oh, what is this?" Sonya's voice leaped at least ten decibels with each word. "I want another!"

"Then you can have another, my sister." Beth slammed her hand down on the bar. "Hey, Matt! Two more specials!"

"Coming right up."

Sonya was already feeling pleasant and warm and tingly from the drink, her cheeks flushing while her lips went numb. Two more shots appeared before them, as if by magic, and this time Sonya didn't need to be talked into it. She threw it down like the pro she was, and after the third shot, she was more than ready to party and dance the night away.

She grabbed her friend by the hand and dragged her out onto the floor, the music moving through her body, the bass thumping and pounding in her veins. Her head was spinning, and she danced like she and Beth were the only ones on the floor. She immediately attracted guys like honey attracts flies, and they swarmed around her, waiting for their turn with the sexy co-eds bumping and grinding their way through song after song, fueled by booze and their own sense of awesomeness.

It was all too easy to pick up drinks from strangers on the floor, but she avoided the offered glasses and straws and made her way back to the bar, her hips gyrating with every step. She ordered another "special" and some mineral water, but when she brought the booze up to her lips, a hand came out of nowhere and plucked the glass from her fingers.

She spun around; furious at whoever the fuck had just jacked her drink. She was ready to give the asshole a piece of her mind but the sight of him literally silenced her. Something tugged at the back of her mind, but she was far too inebriated to pay attention to the warning. He watched her with unfathomably dark eyes, slowly bringing the shot up to his lips and taking a small sip.

"This is shit. Why are you drinking it?"

"It's mine. Why are *you* drinking it?" She demanded hotly, congratulating herself for her clear speech. She reached for her drink, but he held it above his head, easily out of her reach.

"Do you think maybe you've had enough?"

She licked her lips and didn't look away from his bold stare. "Not even close to enough."

"Do me a favor and have a drink of water."

"What are you? My daddy?"

"If I were, I'd turn you over my knee and give you the spanking you so very clearly need."

She blinked, her mouth forming a perfect O. "Excuse me? Who do you think you are?"

He stepped closer, completely invading her space and tilted his head, moving his lips to her ear. She felt his breath over her ear and gave an involuntary shudder. He wasn't touching her, though it felt like he should be. "I think I'm the man who should be your daddy. What about it? Have you been a bad girl?"

"N-no."

"N-no? You don't sound very sure. Now, answer the question. Have you been a bad girl?"

She clutched his tie, pulled his mouth towards her; let her warm breath flutter over his lips. "If you can catch me, I'll tell you anything you want to know."

His reflexes were sharp, but she was young and just a little faster. She spun away from his grasp and shimmied into the crowd, her blonde hair flying around her shoulders as she pushed through the bodies, molding herself against and around them until she was in the middle of the floor again. She spun around, fully expecting to see the handsome stranger just at her heels—men always gave chase—but he wasn't visible through the crowd. She frowned, disappointed, but a strong arm swept around her waist and lifted her feet off the ground.

She shouted with surprise, though nobody heard her above the music, and craned her neck back to see his face. He wasn't smiling. She felt like a child in his arms, his chest a solid wall, the arm around her like a steel band. She kicked her feet fruitlessly, trying to protest between shouts of laughter as he took her away from the crowd. Sonya thought he was just carrying her back to the bar, but he took her past there, down the narrow corridor to a door that said PRIVATE.

He pushed the door open, indifferent to the sign, and kicked it shut behind him. He didn't turn on the light, but enough came in from the windows to light up the desk and chair in the corner. He marched right over to the chair like he owned the place and sat down, flipped her over his lap in a smooth motion.

"What are you doing?" She shouted.

"I'm giving you the spanking you deserve. That was the deal, right? If I caught you?"

"No, no," Sonya gasped out, wiggling against his lap.

She could feel his dick pressing into her stomach, and there was an answering flood of heat between her legs. Did he actually intend to spank her? Nobody had ever done that before—it wasn't something she thought she wanted. Would it hurt? Would he hit her hard enough to leave a mark?

"I just told you I'd tell you what you wanted to know."

"Ah, yes. Well then, answer the question. Are you a bad girl?"

If she wanted to get out of the situation, there was only one answer to give. She should say *no I'm an adult woman and if you don't let me go I'll call the cops*. But what she actually said was, "Yes, sir, I am."

Even though he told her exactly what he was going to do, the slap of his palm against her rounded ass still shocked her. She cried out, her fingers instantly grasping for something. She caught the arm he held her with, digging her fingers into the flexed tendons. *God, he's so strong.* His muscle tone was enough to distract her until he brought his palm down again—this time much harder.

"Son of a bitch!" She yelped.

"Did that sting?"

"Fuck *yes* it did. Fuck. Ow."

"Oh, I didn't hit you that hard. Let me see."

He yanked her short skirt up and her panties down and instead of feeling humiliated or angry, her pussy clenched and her ass tightened. He smoothed his palm over the stinging flesh, rubbing her in gentle circles until the sting faded, replaced by a non-unpleasant tingling. She unconsciously arched her hips and made a sound in the back of her throat, mind, and body agreeing that the attention felt amazing.

"You like that?" He murmured, and the sound of his deep voice went straight to her clit. "Mmm, I think you do."

Goosebumps erupted down her spine and she shivered a little, wiggling her hips. His fingers moved from her thigh to the base of her spine, then slid back down, following the curve of her ass. He squeezed the firm flesh, tickled the sensitive skin, and somehow that made her long for the sting of skin against akin.

Maybe he could read her mind, or maybe she was just lucky enough to want the same thing he wanted, but she did get her wish. He slapped the center of her ass, his palm large enough to sting both cheeks when he brought it down. She jerked and moaned, but the pain was gone before she took her next breath. She pushed her hips up, waiting for his next shot. He didn't disappoint her, and this time the sting didn't fade away. This time it seemed to live inside of her, growing with each breath. She gasped, a strangled sort of whimpering sound, and he immediately resumed his earlier, sweet caresses.

Sonya parted her legs a little wider, and his fingers moved a little lower, dipping between her thighs. She caught her breath as excitement coiled through her, and the first touch of his fingertips on her most sensitive, aroused skin forced the air from her lungs in a sudden, violent exhale. She was so wet that he could easily push his finger into her channel, but he didn't make that obvious move. Instead, he found new ways to torment her, fully exploring her body, touching her in places that nobody had ever really bothered before. She had no idea that the back of her thigh could be so sensitive—or that her nerves were so raw and jumpy along the crease of her thigh. His hands were warm and smooth, his fingers blunt and neatly filed down.

"Open up a little bit more."

She obeyed, clinging all the more tightly to his arm as his thumb brushed over her slit. He massaged the opening, teasing with the tip of his thumb, bringing her up to an impossible level of expectation. She didn't even know what she was doing. Sure, she liked to get her drink on and flirt, but she'd never been dragged into a back office and spanked, and she didn't usually open her legs up to strange men. But it didn't matter that she didn't know this man, she knew what she wanted from him. The big bulge against her stomach was just as arousing as the thumb teasing her folds.

He finally pushed his long thumb into her pussy.

"Fuck..." She moaned. At the same time, he murmured, "You have such a sweet little pussy."

Sonya held herself still at first, though it took everything she had to stop from slamming herself back. She wanted more than just his thumb inside of her. Her walls clenched down, more juices slicking his skin, positively flowing from her as he wiggled the digit around. He slid it free from her body and brought it up to his mouth, licking it like a melting ice cream cone. She watched, equal parts intrigued and frustrated, her pussy fluttering for more attention.

He lifted her without warning, flinging her small frame around like she weighed nothing and settling her on his lap, facing him. She immediately thrust down, grinding her pussy against his hard mound. He moaned, his hands going to her hips.

"Take me out."

She grasped at the zipper with slick fingers and worked it down, shoving her hand into the trousers as soon as there was enough room. She fisted his thick cock and pulled him from his pants, allowing all ten inches of him to stand tall and free. Her eyes widened and she gulped down a sudden fluttering of nerves. She hadn't been with too many other guys, and her last boyfriend had been the record holder at seven inches. And not only was this dick long, but it was also *thick* too. It was perfectly shaped and honestly, beautiful. A clear pearl of pre-cum sat on the tip, and she wiped her thumb over the top and brought it to her mouth to taste his salty essence.

"Suck Daddy's cock," he ordered, not-so-gently pushing on her shoulder.

She slid off his lap and onto her knees, eager to get the most impressive cock she'd ever seen between her lips. Her tongue darted out, again and again, licking away all the pre-cum before she closed her lips around the crown. Her mouth barely fit around him, and she wanted to give herself a chance to adjust to the new sensation against her tongue, but he cupped the back of her head and forced her lower and lower. In what felt like no time at all, she was gagging around his fat head, her tiny mouth and narrow throat over-whelmed by all that thick, throbbing flesh.

"That's good...you're a good little cocksucker...yes you are...look at that..." His hand never left the back of her head, and he controlled the rhythm, pushing against her when she tried to move back up. Everywhere he touched her, she tingled, and the pressure of his fingers sent shock after shock down her spine. She got so caught up in all the sensa-tions flowing through her that she forgot to be over-whelmed, and her last bit of resistance snapped, allowing him to bring her mouth all the way down to his base.

His dick filled her throat, blocking her oxygen and trig-gering her gag reflex. Sonya took deep breaths through her nose, forcing herself to remain calm—she wasn't suffocating and her gag reflex could be overcome. The unfamiliar pres-sure at the back of her throat—and the surprisingly heavy weight against her tongue—ignited more heat, and she pushed her fingers between her wet thighs.

"Oh, you like it that much, hmm? Go on; touch yourself like you want me to touch you. Let me see exactly what you want, little girl."

Goaded by his words, she first pressed two fingers to her clit and grinded them against the throbbing flesh, but that wasn't enough. It felt amazing, the pressure and friction bringing her close to the precipice, but she didn't just want to be close. She wanted to go soaring over the edge so he could see, hear, smell, and even taste, exactly what that was like. She gripped the base of his cock with her free hand and began pumping her mouth back and forth, taking over the rhythm and ignoring the subtle pressure on the back of her head.

She fucked her mouth with his cock, imagining how amazing it would be to ride it instead while she tweaked and pinched and pulled on her swollen clit. The faster she moved, the closer she got, and he was making the most encouraging sounds. Not just words, though she definitely caught those, but long moans and low grunts, too. She couldn't even hear the music throbbing through the club, couldn't hear the people outside their door. She didn't give a second thought to Beth or to the fact that she had to get up very bright and early the next morning.

Quite simply, nothing mattered but this man's dick. *Fuck and I don't even know his name. Oh well. What's in a name, anyway?* Later, she'd definitely remember to ask him for it. And his number, because she would want to definitely want to see this dick again. She swallowed it down hungrily, forgetting that just a few short minutes earlier, she'd been choking and skeptical. Her spit covered his shaft; mingling with the increasing amounts of pre-cum. Would he fuck her until he came in her throat? Would she swallow down his load? She supposed she would if he didn't give her a choice.

The thought was just a stray one, barely touching down in her brain before taking off again, but it was enough to light the final fuse. Something about the thought of being held down and forced to swallow every drop of his jizz hit her right in her core, and her fingers moved furiously over her clit.

"Are you going to cum?"

She moaned out her answer, too far gone to speak even if she didn't have a giant dick in her mouth. He gripped her shoulders, yanked her away from his cock, and picked her up. She yelped in protest, but he ignored her, bringing her down to straddle his lap once again. But he angled and thrust his hips at the last second, filling her in hard stroke that gave her no choice but to take him to the hilt. He felt unlike anybody else she'd ever been with, touched her more deeply than anybody ever had. She doubled over a little, shocked by the pleasure, and then her spine bowed the other direction and she arched back as fireworks of bliss shot through her body.

Once the orgasm started, it didn't stop. It kept rolling forward and then back on itself and then erupting into a new shade of pleasure. She clutched at his shoulders, wrinkling his shirt in her hot, grasping little hands. Everything inside of her clenched tight and she couldn't control the way her muscles tightened or the resulting spasms. She squeezed down around his cock every time he thrust forward, her hips undulating wildly, without any control or check. She couldn't bring herself under control.

A voice of reason broke through her bubble of bliss to remind her that he wasn't wearing a condom. She opened her mouth to voice that thought, but he surprised her by claiming her mouth in a hard kiss, his tongue immediately sliding past her open lips. The voice of common sense retreated, completely ignored as a new fog rolled through her already cloudy brain. His mouth was amazing, the kiss scorching and demanding, and she had no choice but to rise up to the challenge she sensed with each stab and thrust of his tongue.

His grip tightened on her hips, and he moved his own

hips at a harder, faster tempo. She lost her voice, lost her ability to breathe. She buried her face in his neck and tried to brace herself for the final tsunami that was building at that moment. He smelled so good. She wanted to lick him from head to toe. She wanted to roll around on top of him and in his clothes until that smell and permeated her own skin.

"Oh...*fuck*." His cock jerked against her trembling walls, and then she felt a hot flood deep inside of her. She rolled her hips without stopping, pussy clamping down to squeeze out every drop of cum she could coax from him. *At least I'm on the pill.* She would just have to hope this handsome stranger didn't have any terrible surprises for her. *Yeah, and don't be so fucking stupid next time.* That was from what sounded like Beth, and she promised her inner Beth that she wouldn't be so fucking stupid ever again. One time was enough—even with a man as obviously talented as this one.

"That was good. Better than I expected," he said crisply.

She grunted in response, her head still resting on his shoulder. She didn't feel like dancing anymore. In fact, she didn't even feel like returning to the club. He was probably going to head home—and judging by the look of his suit; he had a fine ass home. *No, you can't go with him,* inner Beth reminded her. *You have a job that doesn't even pay your ass, remember? You got to go home!*

Why did Beth have to be right about everything all the time? She wished she could just ignore her inconvenient conscience and sense of responsibility, but that was not an option. Not if she wanted to make a great first impression and dazzle the entire agency until they were all clamoring for her to be made part of the full-time staff.

"Can you give me a ride home?"

"No, but I can call you a cab." He plucked her off his

lap and returned her to her feet. He tugged on her skirt and straightened her blouse, clearly an expert on the cover-up, and then cleaned himself with napkins he found on the desk and tucked his soft cock back into his pants.

"I don't live very far away," she tried.

"I'll cover the fare, too."

That was nice of him, she guessed. Not exactly the sort of generosity she'd been looking for, but she did drink away most of her cash.

"Okay, thanks. What's your name? I'm Sonya, by the way."

"It doesn't matter."

Oh. Well, she supposed that answered her next question. He probably didn't want to exchange numbers. *Fuck, what a fucking bummer. Was it something I did?* She watched as he took his wallet from his pants pocket and opened it. The first thing Sonya noticed was his driver's license.

And the name on his driver's license.

Dominic Barrows.

Of the Barrows Agency.

Her cheeks flared with heat and it suddenly felt like her stomach was trying to make its escape through her throat. She couldn't even wait for him to offer her the cash—all she could do was flee. Flee and hope that he wouldn't have any memory of fucking a Sonya in the back of a club.

Judging by his attitude, she probably didn't have anything to worry about.

She found Beth on the floor and grabbed her by the hand, leading her away from her circle of admirers without a word of explanation.

"What the hell is wrong with you?"

"Are you drunk? Should I drive?"

"What's going on?"

"I just want to get home. Right now." After a shower and a good night's sleep, this wouldn't look so bad. *It'll be fine in the morning.*

But considering what just happened, she had a hard time believing her life would ever be *fine* again.

CHAPTER 2

THE DAY AFTER THE NIGHT BEFORE

SONYA WAKES *up with a pounding headache and enough regret to choke a horse. She wants to quit her internship and crawl back into bed—what else can she do after having a steamy one-night stand with her new boss? But she gathers her courage and goes into the office, hoping that maybe he won't recognize her at all. But he does. And he has no intention of letting her run away.*

"I thought you of all people would support this plan," Sonya said, annoyed and hungover. She sipped from her coffee and winced as the hot liquid burned her tongue. Beth pushed the bottle of creamer at her and shook her head.

"I don't support this plan. It's fucking silly. Why should you resign from your internship because you had a little bit of fun with the boss? If anything, he should be ashamed."

"What if he can't even stand to look at me? Wouldn't it be more embarrassing for him to fire me?"

"You're an intern, Sone. Do you think he's even going to see you? He probably will never realize that the girl he banged at the club is the same one fetching coffee for his secretary."

"I'll be doing more than that," Sonya protested weakly, more out of habit than anything. She figured she'd have some menial, tedious tasks on her list of responsibilities-- well, that's what she used to think. Now she wasn't even sure she wanted a list of responsibilities at the agency. She wasn't actually ashamed of having sex with Dominic Barrows, despite what Beth assumed, but she was worried about the sum total of the rest of her behavior. She'd been completely hammered the night before, she had no sense of shame or reservation, she practically begged him to spank her, and then she really slutted out. She couldn't even say she was acting like another person. She was that party girl, but those days were supposed to be behind her. Hell, that was part of the agreement between her and her father when he pulled the strings to get her the internship.

What if her father found out about what happened? Would Dominic Barrows sell her out like that? The thought made her already upset stomach clench and she groaned, dropping her head on the table.

"This is terrible. I can't do this."

"You don't have a choice. Now finish your coffee and get moving or you're going to be late. Go put on your new outfit, that'll make you feel better."

She was moving as fast as she could, but her limbs were heavy with dread and her head was absolutely pounding. She shuffled to her bedroom and mechanically pulled on the clothes she bought the previous day before they decided to head to the club. Who's the real Sonya? She asked herself ruefully. The twenty-one-year-old woman who bought a sharp suit for the first day of her professional life or the party girl who got wasted and fucked strangers on the night before her big day? She reassured herself she was the professional woman, but she had the sinking feeling that she'd never be anything but the party girl. Maybe she was cursed. Maybe it was in her genes.

Beth was wrong. Wearing her new clothes didn't make her feel better at all. She stared at herself in the full-length mirror not recognizing the woman staring back. Her hand was steady as she applied her make-up, and she expertly covered all the signs of her too-late night and too-stressful morning. She twisted her long hair into a smart bun at the base of her neck, a style that always aged her a good five years. One-inch pumps completed her outfit, and she twirled in front of Beth with no enthusiasm.

"You've got to wipe that glum look off your face, girl. You didn't do anything wrong and nothing bad happened. March in there with your head held high and fetch that coffee like a champion. Come on, smile."

Beth mustered all of her strength to put a smile on her lips, and Beth nodded in approval. "It's not much, but at least you don't look like you're marching off to your own execution."

"Can you drive?"

"Sure. Do you have your lunch money?"

Sonya patted her bag. "Right here." She squared her shoulders. "Let's do this."

The worst thing was that she could not stop thinking about Dominic. His fingers, his mouth, the feel of his breath, and the sound of his voice, every moment of recall made her run hot and cold, and she wished more than anything that she could just shove him out of her mind. She'd had her fair share of drunken hook-ups, and most of the time she barely remembered them the next morning. Mostly because she barely cared to remember them--she loved sex but that didn't mean it was often good. Dominic had paired genuine talent with real skill, playing her body like she was his instrument. He knew exactly where and how to touch, kissed her like he owned her, and when he finally filled her...

She bit her lip and tried to push the memory aside. But she couldn't push it aside because it was everything. She didn't have any other memories or thoughts. Just him. Kissing her. Thrusting into her. Taking his wallet out and inadvertently flashed the truth, throwing a bucket of cold water over Sonya's post-fucking bliss.

Beth tried to pull her from her thoughts as they moved their way through the heavy LA traffic, but Sonya was unresponsive and distracted. Finally, she plugged in her iPod and turned it up, leaving Sonya alone in her silence. Neither one of them spoke until Beth stopped on the corner in front of the skyscraper that housed the agency.

"You need a ride home?"

"Yeah. I'll call you when I'm ready to go." Unless she walked in and handed her resignation. In which case, she'd have all day to make her way back home via bus. And the LA public transportation being what it was, all day was exactly how long it would take.

"Own your shit. Don't let that asshole make you feel sorry to be who you are."

"A slut?"

Beth gave her a hard look. "You know how I feel about that word. Now go do your job."

It won't be that bad, it won't be that bad, it won't be that bad, Sonya repeated to herself again and again as she approached the building. She stopped at the reception desk to give her name and receive her security badge, half convinced the security guard would announce she's not on the list. But he silently handed her the badge, had her sign her name next to the number on his sheet, and then pointed to the elevators behind her. She smiled brightly, but his face didn't shift one iota in response. His name was Tom, according to the tag on his shirt, and she resolved she was going to make him smile, one way or the other. Well, if she ever saw him again after that day.

The Agency took up two floors near the top of the building. She held her breath every time the elevator stopped and the doors opened, convinced that Dominic himself would step between the sliding doors and pin her with hard, knowing eyes. And then maybe pin her with his hard, perfect body. Right up against the wall, giving her no choice but to wrap her legs around his hips while he pushed her skirt up...

Damnit, stop it. Just stop it. Thoughts like that won't make life any easier. Are you trying to sabotage yourself?

Maybe she was. One of her therapists in high school suggested she was self-sabotaging--perhaps due to the fact that she didn't like herself very much. Sonya had straight A's at the time and was working her ass off as class president. She already had a scholarship to UCLA. The therapist's words stung so much that she insisted her mother find her a new doctor or, better yet, stop packing her off to therapy because she was perfectly fine, and normal, and healthy, and NORMAL.

The elevator finally deposited her on the thirtieth floor where giant gold letters on the wall welcomed her to the Barrows Agency. Just the sight of his name was enough to send a tiny thrill down her spine and make her stomach churn with new zest. She stiffened her spine and took measured steps into the reception area where the woman at the front desk offered her a welcoming smile.

"You must be Sonya." She stood and extended her hand.

"I'm Margie and we're so excited to have you here in the office."

Something about Margie soothed her unsettled stomach and she was able to respond with a real smile of her own as she took Margie's hand. "I'm so excited to be here."

"I just need to finish up this email and then I'll give you the big tour. You can wait for me in the employee lounge. It's just through that door. Help yourself to a bagel or some coffee or anything else you like."

The employee lounge was an extremely comfortable-looking room, with two huge couches and several plush chairs. The counter across the back wall had the bagels and coffee Margie mentioned, as well as orange and apple juice, a rack of individually sized cereal boxes, a bowl of fruit, and a box of Krispy Kremes. She absently took a banana from the bowl, rubbing her palm up and down in an unconscious and rather lewd gesture. She peeked her head out from the door to study the office, looking for any familiar faces. She was hoping to see her father, but instead, she was treated to an eyeful of the only other man she called Daddy.

Dominic Barrows was heading right for her.

She panicked and stepped back, but there was no other exit. She was trapped in the lounge, a banana in one hand and a panicked look on her face. Maybe he's on his way to see Margie. She frantically looked around the room for something, anything, to make the situation less awkward. But she couldn't even figure out a way to stand less awkwardly. She tried sitting down, but somehow that seemed even worse. Like she owned the place and she was waiting for him to join her. So she jumped back to her feet just as he walked through the door. She took a deep breath and tried to smile, but he barely looked at her. He made a beeline for the coffee pot and took a giant mug down from the cupboard. He filled it to the brim, sipped the black, bitter liquid, and then turned smartly and walked out again.

Sonya exhaled and sank to the nearest chair, her legs suddenly too weak to support her. That was exactly what she'd hoped would happen, exactly what she needed to happen to keep working at the agency, but somehow it didn't feel like a victory. It felt like a slap to the face. Did he not even recognize her? Did he have no memory of her? Somehow that was more humiliating than any other scenario she'd envisioned. Would he ever remember her? Or would she be an invisible shadow for the next three months? Why couldn't she forget him like he'd obviously forgotten her?

"Sorry that took so long," Margie said as she came into the room. She was probably ten or fifteen years older than Sonya, and she had laugh lines around her mouth and eyes, and she wore her blonde hair in a cute pixie cut. "Did I just see Dominic come in here? Did he say anything?"

"Yes, and no, I don't even think he saw me."

Margie nodded. "Don't worry about that. He doesn't see anybody before he's had his first cup of coffee. He's actually a very good boss. Everybody here loves him."

"I've heard great things about him." And felt even better things. God, how was she ever going to concentrate on her work?

Dominic was the head of the agency, which included three other agents and two lawyers. Sonya's father, Dennis, was one of the lawyers, and she'd met Larry and Angie before, both of whom had visited her parents' house several times. But everybody else was a stranger to her. Margie took her around to each office, and then to the desk of all the administrative and supporting staff, introducing Sonya and explaining who each person was and what they did for the agency. Sonya made careful mental notes, though she feared she'd never remember everybody. Half of her brain was completely checked out, wondering if Margie would introduce her to Dominic. Maybe he was too important to meet the summer intern?

Turned out, that Margie was only saving the best for last.

Dominic's door was partially open--or partially closed depending on what view you took--and Margie gently tapped her knuckles on the solid oak. "Mr. Barrows?"

"Come in."

His voice. Oh God, hearing his voice was so much worse than seeing his face. She felt a cold sheen of sweat on her brow and wiped her clammy palms down the sides of her skirt as Margie led her into the large office. His desk was huge and to Sonya's untrained eye, seemed like a mess of contracts, scripts, and post-it notes. He had two large flat-screen monitors, an iPad, and an iPhone, plus his giant cup of coffee within reach, and he was half-turned from the door, his brow furrowed with concentration while he studied his monitors.

"Get me Drake on the phone, would you? Also, have you heard back from Warner Bros?"

"No, but I can call over there."

"Yeah, do that. I hate it when they drag their feet. Tell them we have plenty of interest in Tony's script, so if they're going to move, they need to do it soon."

"You want me to deliver that message, sir?"

"Sure, why not?" He spun his chair to the left side of the desk and reached for the phone, pausing as he realized that Margie wasn't alone.

"Who is this?"

"This is the new intern, Sonya Rayner."

"Rayner? As in, Dennis?"

"Yes," Sonya said, hoping she didn't sound as nervous as she felt. "He's my father."

"Ah. Good to have you onboard." He pointed at something behind her and said, "You're in charge of that."

Sonya looked over her shoulder to see five huge stacks of envelopes. It looked like a decade's worth of mail saved by the world's biggest hoarder. "What is that?"

"The slush pile. Submissions we didn't ask for. There might be a gem of something in there, but probably not."

Margie gave her a sympathetic look. "We all start at the slush pile. If you can survive that, you can survive anything. Let's see, I can have the stacks moved to the lounge...there should be enough room there to work."

"No, that'll take too much time," Dominic said. "Just have a desk and chair brought in here."

Margie seemed rather alarmed by the suggestion. "Are you sure? It'll be easy enough to get her set up in the lounge so she won't disturb you."

"She's going to be reading terrible scripts for eight hours a day. How will that be disturbing?" He shifted his attention to Sonya, looking her squarely in the eyes for the first time that morning. Her knees went weak. "You don't read out loud or talk to yourself, do you?"

"N-no."

His lip quirked into a small smile, but it was gone as quick as it happened. In fact, Sonya couldn't even be sure she saw it at all. It might have been a trick of the light.

"Have a desk brought in here. We'll make it work."

Margie nodded. "Is there anything else?"

"No, thank you for getting our new girl acquainted with the office. I'll take care of her from here."

And then Margie was gone and Sonya was left alone with him.

"Shut the door, will you?" His attention was on his computer again. She shut the door. "And lock it."

Her pulse spiked and her fingers were trembling as she turned the lock into place. She took a deep breath around her hammering pulse and tried to dry her hands off again. Not even an hour into the day and she was already highly stressed out and shaking. It didn't bode well for a good summer.

"I guess I want to know why you bothered with the show last night if you already had the job."

Sonya spun around, her anxiety quickly replaced by anger. "Excuse me? I didn't...that wasn't about the job. I didn't even know who you were."

He arched his brow skeptically. She closed her hands into fists at her side, digging her fingers into her palm to distract her from the fact that he was the most handsome man she'd ever seen. Why was he running an agency when he could be an actor himself? People would pay to see this man silently read the phonebook to himself.

"Your father has worked here for five years and you had no idea who I was? Hell, there are pictures of me all over the company website."

"I didn't know who you were until I saw your driver's license. Look, I know this is really weird. But if you want me to leave, then let me resign. I'd rather not have to explain to my father why I was fired on my first day."

"Fired? I'm not going to fire you, Sonya. And I'm not going to let you resign, either."

"Um...okay."

"I did tell Margie to bring a desk in here. Why would I do that if I wanted to fire you?"

"I guess you wouldn't."

"Come here."

She shuffled closer to his desk, stopping at the edge. He shook his head and pointed at the space next to him. She didn't want to cross the boundary, though. She wasn't exactly safe anywhere in his office, but she felt less vulnerable with the huge piece of furniture between them. Still, he was her boss and she couldn't just ignore a direct order. Unfortunately, no part of her wanted to ignore his order, even though she was fully aware that the move wasn't without risk.

Sonya circled the desk and stood at his side, eyes nervously jumping back and forth to his beautiful face. He was even more stunning up close. She didn't exactly get a good look at him the night before--another reason why she didn't recognize him. There were too many shadows and the blur from too much booze. But she could see clearly and his face was well-lit by the huge windows behind him. He was in his early forties, but he didn't look any older than thirty. There was no salt in his jet black hair, no wrinkles on his freshly-shaven face, and every inch of his body was pure, muscled perfection. He obviously didn't spend all of his time sitting behind the desk-- or prowling in clubs looking for girls to corrupt in back offices.

"I'm really happy to have the opportunity to work here, but..."

He silenced her by grasping her wrist and yanking her forward, pulling her between his legs. Her pulse jumped again, and the throbbing behind her eyes intensified. There wasn't enough Aspirin in the world for this headache, a result of both the hangover and her elevated, stressed state. He held her attention with his eyes as he dragged his fingers up the side of her thigh, pushing her skirt higher and higher up her leg.

"Stop it," she whispered.

"Why?"

"Because that's not...that's not why I'm here."

"Isn't it?"

"No!"

"That's not what I think. I think you knew exactly who I was and I think you got...you're getting...exactly what you want."

She shook her head, but she didn't push his hand away. She couldn't look away from him, either. She felt like she was being hypnotized. The night before she could blame the alcohol on her spaced-out reaction, but now there was nothing and nobody to blame but him. His fingers were still traveling up her thigh, and he smiled the moment he made contact with her damp panties. The brief pressure of his fingertips was enough to make her shudder and widen her stance, her body already anticipating his demanding touch.

"There's no reason to deny it," he murmured. "We're both consenting adults, aren't we? We can share a few minutes of pleasure..."

That wasn't quite right, but for the life of her, she couldn't explain why. He pushed her panties away from her mound, fingers gliding between her swollen lips, and it was like he never stopped touching her at all. She gasped, her hips rocking forward as his blunt nail moved over her clit. The small bud of flesh jerked, swelling and pulling tight. He put his arm around her, holding her close against his chest while he reangled his hand, allowing two fingers to slide into her hot channel.

Her hand flew to her mouth and she bit down to keep from crying out, the pleasure so intense that she saw stars in front of her eyes. He thrust into her with hard, short strokes, twisting his hand so he hit her G-spot directly. She had no choice but to grasp his shoulders, her weak knees bending, her head swimming. The sound of his fingers moving against her moist flesh was loud in the room, growing louder as she coated his fingers with her juices. She tried to swallow back her moans of pleasure, tried to choke them all down, but there was nothing she could do to dampen them as he twisted his fingers inside of her, grinding them back and forth, pushing them deeper until it felt like he was touching the back wall of her pussy. Then she had no choice but to kiss him, sealing her lips to his in a desperate, moaning kiss.

He tasted like coffee and mint, and he welcomed her questing tongue, licking over her lips before invading her mouth with his own tongue. She pressed even closer, her hips rocking against his hand as the sensation intensified, building into a bigger and bigger wave. She could feel his cock against her thigh, and she pressed to his shaft until he finally responded and began rocking against her. They were like a couple of teenagers grinding and panting against each other. She'd walked away from their earlier encounter half convinced she would never feel anything that amazing again, but she was already rushing headlong into an orgasm that threatened to rival the fireworks from the night before. Maybe it was because he was finding her most sensitive spot with every powerful thrust. Or maybe it was because it was even more illicit, with the entire staff, including her father, just on the other side of the door. Or maybe it was because she was sober and there was no booze dulling her senses or fogging her mind.

It started at the bottom of her feet. She felt a strange tingling, a sensation that something was being pushed up from her very toes. She clenched, bracing herself for the tidal wave that would follow as the pleasure climbed higher and higher, flowing up her spine and spreading down every vein and into every inch of her body. She gasped against his mouth, making a strangled sound of warning and surprise, and he cupped the back of her neck and massaged the tender tendons at the base of her skull. The tension down her back suddenly disappeared, as though he flipped a switch to release the tight muscles, allowing the pleasure to wash through her without obstacle.

He swallowed her shouts down as the orgasm hit her with the full force of a hurricane, her entire body shaking while she drenched his hand with a flood of her cum. He groaned and pushed against her thigh and she realized that she wasn't the only one who'd been overwhelmed by the situation. That was another first--she'd never made a guy cum in his pants like that. She hadn't even touched him, though when she looked down she realized there was more than one stain on his expensive pants. The room smelled like sex--her sex, specifically.

"Uh...I'm sorry...about your pants," she stammered, more than a little horrified.

He shook his head and gently eased his fingers from her slick pussy. Her walls clenched down at the loss and it was all she could do not to straddle his lap and demand his cock.

"I've got other pants. Don't worry about it. There's a bathroom." He pointed to the door behind him. "Go get yourself cleaned up. And Sonya? Don't mention leaving again. You're not going anywhere."

"Yes, sir." What else could she say? Where else would she want to be? And how soon could they do that again? Very soon, she hoped.

Very, very soon.

CHAPTER 3

SWEET DISPOSITION

SONYA IS ALREADY HAVING *a bad day when Fiona, Dominic's girlfriend, strolls through the office like she owns the place. First Dominic yells at her for no reason and then his stuck-up bitch of a girlfriend throws her water in Sonya's face for no reason. Angry and humiliated, Sonya never expects Dominic to apologize. Oh, he doesn't say the words, but he doesn't have to.*

"What is this?"

At first, Sonya didn't realize Dominic was speaking to her. He rarely spoke to her during the day and she was accustomed to tuning out his voice so it wouldn't interrupt her work.

"Sonya? Anybody home? I asked you a question."

She jerked her attention from the script she was reading and spun in her seat to face him. He held a script clenched in one hand, wrinkling all the pages, and his eyes were hard as twin black stones.

"I'm sorry, sir." When he made her nervous that word always slipped in, completely unwelcome and completely unconscious. "I didn't hear the question."

"What. Is. This?" He hit it with his left hand on the last syllable, his face almost thunderous.

Sonya jumped from her chair and crossed the room to inspect the offending paper. She had no idea what he was holding, or why he was demanding an explanation from her. He threw it at her without a word, nearly hitting her in the face with the thick manuscript. She caught it and nearly fumbled it from her fingers before catching sight of the title, "One Headlight." She recognized--it was the first script she actually read from start to finish. The slushpile was brutal, full of garbage, some of which she couldn't even read past the first few lines. But "One Headlight" had caught her attention and held it, and so when she finished reading it, she filled out the appropriate form, stapled into the top of the script, and put it in Dominic's inbox.

And now he was looking at her like he could beat her to death with the script in question. She didn't understand the problem, but it was clear she'd done something wrong.

"It's a script that I thought you would enjoy reading."

"You thought wrong," he bit out. "And who asked you to give me things you think I'd enjoy? You don't know my tastes, for one thing. For another, I'm not in this business for pleasure. Do you understand me?"

"I...I don't know."

"Well, it's pretty easy. I'm in the business to make money. Do you really think this script could make any money?"

"I thought it was a great read and I can see it becoming a movie." Did he expect her to stand up for herself and her choices? Or was she supposed to lower her head deferentially and apologize for making such a terrible mistake?

"Oh, you can see it becoming a movie? I'm sorry; I didn't

realize that you honeymooned as a studio exec. Or are you a producer?"

She was sorry for upsetting him before, but now she was mostly getting annoyed. Her spine straightened and her hackles went up. "If you don't think I'm capable of recognizing a well-written script, then why am I in charge of the slush pile?"

"You're not in charge of anything. I am in charge of everything. And I never said that your job was to refer scripts to me. Your job is to send out the rejections."

"But what if I find something good?" And regardless of what he thought, "One Headlight" was a great script. Quirky, funny but dramatic, serious, and real.

"You won't find anything good. And I didn't tell you to find anything good. All you need to do is send out the rejection letters, got it?"

"Yes, sir. So...does that mean I don't even have to read all the submissions?"

"You don't have to read any of them, really. I'm not interested in taking on anybody new right now."

"How do you get your clients?"

"I have plenty of clients. When I want another, I'll ask one of them for referrals."

"So it really is who you know."

"Says the young lady who only got the job because her father handles my international rights and foreign markets. I guess life is pretty sweet when you know all the right people."

Sonya didn't have a quick answer for that. Before she could think of one, the door flew open and a feminine but surprisingly low voice said, "Darling, you really must fire that worthless receptionist of yours."

Dominic instantly stood, and Sonya spun around to

see who the interloper was. She didn't recognize the woman as having ever been in the office before, and she definitely had the sort of body and face that she wouldn't forget. Her hair hung down to her waist in a straight, shiny curtain, and she wore a very expensive green dress that flattered her figure and her complexion. Matching white pumps and a handbag completed the look, and she sauntered into the room with an easy sway of her hips. Sonya couldn't tell her age--it could have been as young as twenty-one or as old as forty. Her face was flawless and unwrinkled, but there was something almost world-weary about her, and she barely noticed Sonya as her eyes flicked around the room. She certainly didn't acknowledge her or do anything to indicate she knew she wasn't alone with Dominic.

Dominic circled the desk and pulled her against him in a warm embrace, then kissed each cheek briefly before placing a longer, lingering caress on her full, painted lips. The woman smiled up at him as he lifted his head, and Sonya took an unconscious step back, and then another. She needed to put as much space between them as possible because this was clearly the girlfriend. And women had a special sixth sense when it came to cheating--though she had the feeling she would be on the shit-list regardless of her guilt or innocence. But she was definitely not innocent, and she wanted to make her escape before this woman figured that out.

"Margie has been with me since I opened my doors, Fiona. This place could no more run without her than it could without me," Dominic pointed out reasonably.

She gave a little sniff of disbelief. "I find that very doubtful. What does she do other than incompetently answer the phone and slowly fetch coffee?"

"You didn't come all the way down here to complain about Margie, did you?"

"No, actually. I was having lunch with my dear friend Judy. She told me her husband is searching for a new agent. His current agent isn't as honest or as aggressive as he would like."

"Judy?" Dominic tilted his head and frowned. "Judy Macklin? Wife of Frank Macklin?"

"Yes."

"The Frank Macklin."

"Yes." She glanced over to where Sonya was still standing, silent and more confused than ever. "I need a tall glass of ice water and something for this headache. I don't want a bottle of water, it must be in the glass, and don't forget the ice."

Her tone made it clear that she expected no argument, and Dominic didn't even bother to speak up and explain that Sonya read scripts, she didn't fetch water. With no choice, she excused herself from the office and crossed the floor to the break room. There weren't any glasses, but she did find a plastic cup that she filled with ice and water. She rummaged through the First Aid kit until she found a small packet of Tylenol and quickened her step, returning just in time to interrupt some heavy kissing and groping.

Sonya took an involuntary step back at the sight, a small "Oh" escaping her lips. Of course, he'd have a girlfriend. She shouldn't have been surprised by the fact. And of course, she would be perfect for a man as powerful and wealthy as Dominic. She cleared her throat softly and squared her shoulder, approaching as Dominic lifted his head.

"Here you go," Sonya said brightly like the loved doing nothing more than serving entitled bitches with cold water.

"What's this?" Fiona asked with a blank look.

"The water and Tylenol you asked for." What the hell? Was this some sort of joke? Or a test?

Fiona took the plastic cup from her, considered it for a moment, and then threw the full contents at Sonya's face, drenching her with the ice-cold liquid. She gasped for breath and tensed, her hair plastered to her scalp, her clothes drenched.

"I said I wanted a glass of water. Not some children's cup. Now go find me a glass."

Sonya looked over to Dominic, the plea in her eyes obvious. She had work to do, and she would much rather get back to that than continue to suffer indignities at this strange woman's hands.

"Why don't we go to lunch?" Dominic interjected smoothly, putting his arm around her waist. She nodded, relaxing against his much larger body, content and confident in her place at his side. "Sonya has a lot of work to do."

That was all he said. No apologies. No assurances that she could go home. He didn't even ask if she was okay. She didn't wait for another word from him before rushing off to the bathroom to stare at her own shocked face in the mirror. Her hair was ruined, her make-up was running, and she just hoped her business suit wasn't stained or ruined. She was drying her face with a wad of paper towels when Margie slipped into the room and gave her a sympathetic look.

"I should have warned you about Fiona. But when she's not here, I do my best to not think about her at all. I'm much happier when I pretend she doesn't even exist."

"Who is she? She's horrid!"

"She's his girlfriend. They've been together for...oh years now."

"Years? Why on earth would he want to be with her for years? She's a brat. And a bitch. Not a good combination."

"She has plenty of attractive assets to offset her bratty bitchiness. Fortunately, she doesn't come around the office often."

Sonya screwed up her face. "I suppose he's getting what he deserves. I doubt she's pleasant and reasonable when they're together."

"Nah, she's a spoiled brat. Her daddy was a pretty high-level exec at MGM and she grew up thinking she had her run of Hollywood. Do you want to go home for the day?"

Sonya sighed and threw the paper towel away. "No. There's only a few hours left and he probably won't come back today, will he?"

"No, probably not."

"I have a question about the scripts I'm reading...what should I do if I like any of them?"

"Put it in my inbox. If it's something Dominic should see, I'll make sure it gets in front of him. That's one reason I don't have to worry about my job security around here. I've got a good eye and I've made him a lot of money over the years."

Sonya nodded. "Okay, I'll do that from now on."

"Did he tell you to send everybody a rejection?"

"Yes. And most of the scripts do deserve a rejection, but there are a few gems in there. And that doesn't seem fair to them."

"I agree. Don't worry, I've got you covered." She smiled sympathetically. "Really, nobody will think less of you if you need to go home after your first run in with the she-beast."

"No, no, I'm good. I don't look like a drowned rat, do I?"

"Not at all."

Margie walked her back to Dominic's office. It was always strange for Sonya to be left in there by herself. She had access to his entire desk and all of his files. She could go snooping through his drawers and she was pretty sure she already knew his password. But she never did anything like that. When he left her, she stayed at her desk, ignoring the temptation that his entire office offered. The temptation was even greater now, especially since she was full of vindictive anger at his bitchy girlfriend. But she didn't give in to that temptation and she was very glad of her self-control when he strolled through the door two hours later, closing and locking it behind him.

She blanched as she heard the lock click into place. Did he really want to have sex with her after what just happened? He didn't even demand she apologizes. Was Sonya really worth so little to him that he thought he could stand by while she was humiliated and talked down to and then just fuck her whenever he felt like it? It may not have been completely obvious to him, but she had a good deal more self-respect than that.

He didn't return to his desk. He walked over to stand in front of her chair, and she had to crane her neck up to meet his eyes. He was much taller than her anyway, and now he was positively looming over her. He reached down, brushing a damp strand of hair from her face. He caressed her cheek with his thumb, the simple touch so gentle that it almost made her forget she was damned angry--and had every right to be damned angry. She flinched away from his touch, narrowing her eyes and shooting daggers at him, hoping he could see that she was very much not amused or impressed.

Rather than being deterred by her irritation, he dropped to his knees in front of her. He put his hands on her knees and forced them apart, his eyes locked on her face, challenging her to break the eye contact—or push him away. Her nostrils flared as she took a deep breath and she put a foot against his chest, but she didn't kick him back. Didn't do anything to put any distance between them.

He pushed his fingers up her thighs, hiking her skirt up higher and higher until he could see her panties. She'd gone out the previous weekend and bought the finest, softest silk panties—ones she couldn't really afford but made her feel very sexy. Why she wanted to feel very sexy beneath her professional suits, she didn't even dare explain to herself. Today she wore red ones, and he slid his hands under her ass and pulled her forward on the chair, angling her hips and dipping his head. He dragged his tongue over the silk crotch of her panties, the heat of his mouth scorching her through the thin material.

"What..." *What do you think you're doing?* The words were right there, the angry question dancing on the tip of her tongue, but it was obvious what he was doing. Her body certainly wasn't confused. Desire immediately flooded her body, and the next time he licked over her swollen lips, her panties were completely damp. By the third time, the silk was soaked through with her juices and her temperature was rising. He hadn't even touched her skin directly and she was already feeling short of breath.

"You can't just—"

"Yes, I can," he said calmly, his mouth moving over her as he spoke. He exhaled through his lips, blowing a cool stream of air over her mound.

"No, I..."

He hooked his fingers around the silk panties and gently pulled them down her thighs, pushing them all the way to her feet, unhooking them from her ankles. He casually stuffed them in his jacket pocket, and she began to protest again, but this time he wasn't playing. He cut off her words —and any thoughts she might have been trying to process—

by burying his tongue between her lips, lapping at the slick petals until she was literally gasping for breath. His warm hands glided up her calves and he lifted her by the knees, hooking her legs over his shoulders. She automatically locked them in place, using her grip to pull him even closer to her throbbing pussy.

What are you doing? You can't be so weak! He needs to know this isn't okay!

Sonya agreed with that voice. She really did. But what could she do about it now that his face was buried between her legs? He wasn't going to stop and did she really want to pull his hot mouth, his clever tongue from her throbbing flesh? Her clit was already swollen, aching for his attention, and her pussy walls were clenching, fresh fluids slipping from her with every flutter and contraction.

He moved his mouth with slow deliberation, lapping the juices away from her labia until she was squirming against his face, pressing her pussy to his mouth, riding his tongue as he dipped it into her channel. He wiggled it around as if trying to coax more of her sweet arousal down the back of his tongue, awaking all her nerve-endings, fanning the flames in her lower stomach. She unconsciously lifted her hands to her breasts, tweaking her hard nipples between her thumbs and forefingers. Her skin responded by growing tauter, more sensitive, and spikes of pleasure shot straight from her nipples to her clit, which twitched against Dominic's nose as he dipped his tongue into her again and again.

He didn't move quickly. He wasn't in any sort of hurry. His tongue was long and smooth, and each time he filled her, it awakened a desire for something much larger, much harder. She bit her tongue, pressing her lips together so she wouldn't beg him to fuck her, wouldn't blurt out all of her desperate desire. She dreamed about him at night; he was the first thing she thought about in the morning and the last person she pictured before she went to sleep. She was almost in a constant state of arousal, her desire for him only growing the longer she spent in his presence.

And now, even when she had several good reasons to be angry at him, her body was too greedy, too hungry for it, to ever allow her to voice a single one. The only words her mouth would allow were pleas, and her irritation didn't truly spike to anger until he lifted his head, leaving her bereft of his tongue, hollow and aching.

"Please," she moaned, dropping her head back. The ceiling spun above her, moving in faster and faster circles while her heart pounded in her ears. "Please, please, please."

"Please?"

His tone was almost mocking, but she didn't care. He dipped his head and this time he caught her clit between his lips. He sucked gently, coaxing more and more blood to her already swollen and dripping pussy. She tilted her hips and rocked them back and forth and he responded by flicking his tongue over the extra-sensitive tip. She bit down on the back of her hand to keep from howling, the sensation hovering between pleasure and pain. She was too sensitive, far, far too sensitive. She felt raw, felt like all her nerve-endings were exposed, and no matter how she rocked and swiveled her hips, she couldn't get the relief she was looking for, the contact she craved. He kept her hanging in that terrible limbo, her lungs seized, her heart pounding so hard it could have leaped right from her chest.

"Uhmmmmm...please...please..." She couldn't be left in that terrible space forever. She needed more of something. Or she needed less of something. She needed to be pushed over the edge or pulled back from the brink, but she was afraid she'd go insane, or simply explode, if he kept her hanging there.

But he wasn't a complete monster. He took pity on her, sliding one finger up and down her slit before pushing the tip against her opening. He smeared her juices around the entrance and over his finger before guiding one digit deep inside. He pumped his hand slowly, working her open without hitting that magic spot that would have her climbing the walls. She caught her breath though. She knew it was coming.

Dominic repositioned his mouth, angling his chin and sucking harder on her clit. She jerked her hips like he touched her with a live wire, and he chose that moment to press into her G-spot. She had to bite down with bruising strength on the back of her hand to keep from howling, and her hips went insane. The switch inside of her brain had been thrown—or maybe the switch was in her hips. Wherever it was, she was no longer in control of her body or responsible for her actions. On the next thrust, he was stretching her with two fingers, and she was yearning for far more than that.

He alternated between flicking his tongue over her clit and grinding it down into the tender flesh. She moaned and yipped, unsure what felt better, what she needed more. She rolled her hips and he doubled down on her clit, sucking hard enough to make her see stars. Her breath caught in her throat, and her teeth sank even deeper into the flesh on her arm. If she wasn't careful, the whole office—including her own father!—would know everything that was going on behind that locked door. And it felt so fucking good in that moment that she didn't even care.

Dominic moved his hand faster, sawing his fingers in

and out quickly, increasing the pressure around her clit. She began to thrash, the pleasure building up inside of her, starting in her core and spreading through her limbs and up to her head. The shortness of breath and lack of oxygen was getting to her, and she felt a familiar twinge below the pads of his fingers—the sign that her orgasm was imminent. In the next second, rockets of bliss shot up her spine and she went rigid as the fireworks erupted. Her hips moved all the faster, her movements becoming frantic and as soon as the first orgasm washed through her, she was plunged into another one. She swam through the waves of pleasure, surfacing long enough to gasp for breath, and then she was overcome by another crashing wave.

Her clit jerked rapidly against his tongue, and that friction alone was enough to plunge her beneath the breakers again and again and again. Her G-spot felt swollen and tender, and she was sure he added a third finger. Finally, she felt as though she was being torn apart and the final wave was the greatest of all, knocking her over the head and stealing what was left of her breath.

"Please," she whimpered. "I need...I need to breathe...I can't..."

She almost expected him to ignore her, but he eased up and she slumped back in the chair, shaking and exhausted. He turned his head, gently kissing her trembling thighs until the aftershocks had worked through her system. Only then did he sit back on his heels and gaze up at her. She watched him from beneath her lashes, her eyelids heavy and low. She couldn't say anything. Even if she had something to say, her mouth wouldn't cooperate. Nothing would. She was completely spent and watery.

"Take the rest of the afternoon off, hmm?"

For some reason, the first words she could find were a

rushed apology. "I'm sorry about the script, I didn't realize—
"

He shook his head. "Don't worry about it. And if you need to replace that blouse, you can just submit the receipt for reimbursement."

"Oh. Okay. Thank you."

Dominic pushed himself to his feet and licked his lips, a small smile of satisfaction temporarily crinkling his eyes. "It's no problem. Enjoy the rest of your day off."

That sounded like a direct order. She obeyed automatically. Nobody else had this control over her, not even her father, but when Dominic spoke she almost always jumped to obey. She stood and pulled her skirt down, but didn't ask for her panties back. He returned to his chair, propping his feet up on his desk and resting his iPad on his lap. She recognized his frown of concentration, so she gathered up her purse and let herself out the door without another word.

She waved at Margie as she passed, but didn't stop to speak to her. She was afraid the older woman would somehow know she was leaving her boss's office *sans* panties like the truth was stamped all over her flushed face.

CHAPTER 4

GET DOWN AND GET LOW

IT'S *the end of the first month and Sonya and Dominic have an understanding and a mutually beneficial routine, but she doesn't know what she is to him. She realizes that they probably only have two months together and the thought makes her strangely sad. Feeling brave and curious, she takes the initiative for once...but how will he respond if he's not the aggressor?*

The slush pile wasn't as bad as Sonya thought it would be--it was worse. Much worse. At first, she vowed she would read all the submissions in their entirety, out of respect for the artist who submitted it. She hated the thought of discounting an entire script because the first few pages were bad. She was a fast reader, but she had all summer and that was her only assignment. Well, not her only assignment, but it was the only thing anybody else knew about. However, after only a week in Dominic's office, Sonya had completely given up on the noble idea of investing her time in every piece of trash she picked up. The vast majority of submissions were terrible--offensive, confusing, racist, misogynistic, too broad, too narrow, too many misspellings, too much "creative formatting," and even a handful of abusive letters. The letters were the most perplexing to her. They wanted Dominic to work for them and with them, yet they introduced themselves with a barrage of passive-aggressive insults, veiled accusations of nepotism, and declarations that all the work done in Hollywood was hackneyed shit.

Everybody was right. It really only took one page. By the time she got to the bottom of the first one, she knew if she would be sending back the standard rejection letter--a brief, neutral message expressing the unfortunate fact that the agency wasn't searching for clients at this time and adding that they hoped the screenwriter had the greatest success with his search. If she could make it through the first ten pages, she'd set it aside in another pile for later consideration. She didn't know much about making movies, and until that assignment, she'd never seen a screenplay treatment, but she wasn't stupid. She could definitely tell quality when she saw it.

Sometimes she wished that Margie had moved the slushpile out to the lounge. That way, she could work in peace without the constant distraction that was her boss. He didn't talk to her much, but he didn't have to speak in order to be distracting. His expensive cologne tickled her nose. He was constantly taking calls and even if the content was vague or boring to her, his voice always aroused her interest. She angled herself so she could watch him from the corner of her eye and she always felt an uncomfortably sharp stab of disappointment when he left the office for one of his endless lunch meetings or golf games.

He was a busy man. The whole office worked in perfect harmony to keep everything running smoothly, and though a different emergency seemed to crop up every day, he never broke stride—he didn't even sweat. Sonya felt like she was learning far more than she ever dreamed possible. The slushpile might be a painful waste of time, but every day Dominic taught her something new about running an agency, handling clients, or smoothing things over after a rough meeting.

She also learned how much pleasure can be added to any given day, and in fact, how easy it was to mix business and pleasure.

"Lock the door." Those three little words were often the only words he spoke to her during the day. Sometimes she wondered if he even remembered she was there. Other times she wondered if he even liked her—if he even thought of her as a person at all. Or was she just the office slave and kinky sex toy? The girl who was supposed to scratch his itch? And when she started asking those sorts of questions, she wondered how she allowed herself to get to that position at all. Shouldn't she have more self-respect than that? But those questions, and any sense that she should have more self-respect, disappeared immediately whenever he'd loosen his tie and order her to lock the door.

The words had an automatic affect on her. Her heartbeat quickened, her pulse spiked, and the air rushed out of her lungs. She felt clammy and cold and hot all at once, and her fingertips and toes tingled with anticipation. Her pussy clenched, and blood rushed to her labia and clit, so that by the time he got her panties off her, her pussy was swollen and sloppy with juices. Her nipples hardened. Her cheeks flushed. The room felt a little spinny and the vague fear of being caught, of her father finding them even though the door was locked, sending sparks of heat racing up and down her spine.

When he said them, she immediately set aside whatever terrible script she was reading, calmly rose from her chair, and turned the doorknob lock into place. The click of the lock had almost the same effect as the sound of his voice—just another small way to ratchet up the tension and antici-pation. She'd smooth her damp palms out on her skirt and try to look normal, try to smile and be calm, but she knew she never looked as calm as him. Most of the time, he didn't even look like a man who was about to have sex.

Of course, once they got started he was passionate and demanding, hungry and hard. She felt like she was caught up in his whirlwind, and she couldn't even catch her breath until after he left her tired and boneless and completely drained of energy. After a month of this, she wasn't even close to tired of it. If anything, she wanted more. She not only wanted more from him, but she also wanted to give him more. She loved to hear him moan, loved to catch the soft sounds of his pleasure, loved to witness the bliss flut-tering over his handsome face as pleasure completely over-took him.

Since being in the same room as him was enough to make her horny, it was only a matter of time before she grew impatient waiting for those words and decided to take matters into her own hands. That fateful day came on the last Friday of the month she began her internship. He'd been out of the office for the previous three days, traveling with one of his actors on a press junket, and he only stopped in long enough for a conference call with Warner Bros that couldn't be rescheduled.

Dominic strolled into the office without sparing her a second glance. He didn't even greet her, just shrugged off his jacket and crossed to his desk. Margie was hot on his heels, a cup of coffee in hand, and she quickly made sure that the boss man was caffeinated, comfortable, and dialed into the call. When she left, Sonya stood, crossed to the door, and locked it without waiting for him to issue the order himself. He didn't seem to notice, as the call was beginning and he was going through the standard greetings.

She nervously licked her lips and approached his desk, her heart hammering with wild excitement. *What if he doesn't want me to take the initiative? What if it pisses him off? What if he throws me out?* And that was just the tip of the iceberg when it came to her fears and concerns, but that didn't stop her from rounding his desk to stand at his side. She gripped the back of his leather chair and spun it so he was facing her. His brows knitted together in a silent question, but he looked more confused than irritated.

Sonya chose to interpret that as a great sign.

She hiked her skirt up around her thighs and lowered herself to her knees between his legs. He obligingly spread them wider, still looking at her with an expression of utter confusion. It almost made her want to laugh. Why did he seem so confused by what was going on? Wasn't it obvious what she was doing? And what she wanted?

She pulled at his fly, drawing his zipper down slowly. He had plenty of opportunities to swat her hand away, push her aside, or spin the back of the chair toward her. But he seemed completely wrapped up in his conversation as if he wasn't even aware of what she was doing and had even less interest in the possibilities. She didn't let that discourage her, though. She pushed her hand into his pants and wrapped her fingers around his thick cock.

He wasn't fully erect, but he was definitely showing some interest. She tightened her grip and stroked from the tip to the base, then leaned forward and closed her mouth around the mushroom head. She ran her tongue along the ridge, licked over the top as though he was a lollipop, and coaxed drops of clear liquid onto the tip of her tongue. She glanced up from beneath her lashes to watch his face, but he was still impassive, his voice completely even as he responded. The meeting was still going well, but they would be talking about numbers soon, and that's when everybody's blood pressure skyrocketed.

The longer she sucked on the head, the harder he got until he was at full mast. His cock was heavy on her tongue and her lips were stretched into a tight ring around his thick shaft. She lowered her head incrementally, sliding her mouth down until she reached the base of his shaft. Sonya closed her eyes, shivering with delight as his earthy musk filled her nose. She could taste him on the back of her tongue, too, and the salty hint drove her to push her mouth against his base, burying her nose in his short, soft curly hair.

He rested his hand on the back of her head, his palm warm and gentle on her scalp. She tensed, waiting for him to push her away, or push her down so he filled her throat even more completely, but he wasn't trying to guide her. He was just holding her, reminding her through touch that he was the boss since sound wasn't an option. But she didn't need the reminder at all. She knew her place, knew to do what he wanted her to do. She pulled back slightly, and he allowed her to slide his cock down her tongue and out of her mouth. She swiveled the tip of her tongue around his head, teasing the most sensitive skin until the flesh jerked against her lips as if demanding entry into the hot depths once again.

Sonya's gaze returned to his face, and now his eyes were locked on her, his earlier confusion completely replaced by the hungry look she knew so well. She knew what he wanted from her, knew what his flesh was throbbing for, but she wasn't going to simply swallow him down her throat.

For once, she was the aggressor, she was the one acting first, and she had the upper hand. That would change the second he ended his call, she had no doubt about that. Dominic Barrows was a man accustomed to being in charge.

Sonya dragged the tip of her tongue up and down his shaft, painting it with her saliva, coating him until his skin was good and slick. She fisted his cock and stroked from the tip down, spreading the pre-come, smearing it across his flesh. She slid her partly opened mouth along the underside of his shaft, teasing him with heat but not enveloping him. She knew he could feel it, knew there were tremors racing through his limbs. She could even feel the slight trembling in his thighs.

She pulled his pants down lower so she could grip the bare skin of his upper legs, her fingers pressing into his well-muscled thighs. Dominic took great pride in his body and his appearance and worked hard to maintain his chiseled body. She'd never seen him at the gym, but a part of her was dying to follow him there one night after work and watch him sweat his way through a grueling workout. She wanted to see his skin slick with sweat, wanted to see his muscles straining and his face tight with effort and concentration. But at the moment, she could only imagine how hard he worked out by feeling how hard his muscles were.

"Yes, but the deal...will you please stop interrupting me?" The note of irritation in his voice automatically made her stop, but he increased the force of his touch, keeping her mouth low on his shaft. "Thank you. Now, as I was saying, the deal could be quite lucrative for the studio in the long run. But you have to be reasonable about this. We're talking about a man's livelihood."

His voice was so even, so controlled. The best thing about Dominic was his control—it was exceptional, no matter what he was doing. She wanted to break through that control. Wanted to be good enough—exceptional enough in her own way—to completely bust down all of his defenses. She wanted to hear a ragged moan, wanted to make his voice crack with desperation.

She redoubled her efforts, sealing her lips around his swollen head and sucking hard, her tongue lightly flicking over the sensitive tip. He shifted slightly, moving forward in his seat and arching his hips. She hollowed her cheeks, increasing the pull until he made a sound deep in his throat and tried to cover it with a small cough to clear his throat.

"What's that? Sorry, my phone...uh huh...right."

She formed a tight fist at his base, squeezing the firm flesh in her palm while she bobbed her head, adding friction to the pressure and suction. His fingers curled on the back of her scalp, tangling in her hair and he pulled slightly. Not hard enough to hurt, but enough to send a cascade of chills down her spine, her pussy clenching in immediate response. She squeezed her thighs together, trying and failing to relieve the throbbing that was increasingly demanding her attention.

He nudged a foot between her thighs and she pushed her crotch against his toes, gratefully grinding against his shoe as she sank her mouth lower and lower. She released her hold on his shaft and relaxed her mouth, accepting his full length all the way down the back of her throat. He held her down, fingers alternately pressing and massaging her tender scale, occasionally shocking her with a hard pull right at the roots.

She didn't move for a long, long time once he was lodged in the back of her throat. She took deep breaths through her nose, concentrating on breathing when her gag reflex tried to reject the weight settled in her throat. He lifted his hips slightly, dropped them down, and then lifted them again, rocking forward urgently. She felt a thrill of satisfaction at the short, sharp thrusts, but he was still breathing normally, still talking normally.

Sonya began bobbing her head, pressing her hands down on his thighs while she fucked her mouth with his cock. She moved faster and faster, jaw relaxed and throat opens as she took him deep down her passage.

"If you're not willing to make a deal, then I'm not sure what else I have to say. Uh-huh...uh huh...uh..." He swallowed hard, hips rising even further as he got carried away with the momentum. His words were slightly winded, frayed at the ends, and Sonya didn't know if anybody else would notice, but she heard it loud and clear. It was what she'd been waiting for, after all.

"Talk to him and get back to me," he said his voice curt. It was clear that he wanted the phone call to be over, and he didn't even wait for a response before he slammed the phone down. With both hands free, he cupped her head between his palms and now he was completely in charge, free to slam his hips forward as hard as he wanted.

While he was on the phone, they'd both done a great job of keeping quiet, but now there was nothing to stop her low moans of pleasure as he slammed into her throat. He grunted with each thrust, building speed, building friction, using her mouth ruthlessly, like he didn't care if she liked it. It wasn't about what she wanted, only his undeniable satisfaction.

She shifted, grinding faster and faster against the bottom of his foot, using the pressure and friction to her advantage. She felt the heat building beneath her skin, felt the flush along her limbs and down her spine, behind her eyes. She lifted her gaze, drinking in the sight of him with his tie askew and his eyes closed. He must have felt her staring at him because his eyes snapped open, and she was caught in the twin abyss of his dark, burning eyes. They were perfect, coal-dark ring of blackness, but she saw something burning behind them—she felt it too. Whatever fire raged inside of him was already hot enough to scald her.

Sonya slammed her hips forward, pressing her clit hard against his shoe. He pointed his toes downward, driving the end even more into her tender flesh and it was like touching a raw, vulnerable nerve—or more like punching it with a fist of fire. The orgasm tore through her, ripping her apart, distracting her completely from the task at hand. But he wasn't distracted, and while she trembled and shook from the force of the impact, he buried himself in her throat one final time and flooded it with shot after shot of his come.

She swallowed it down because she had no choice, her hips gyrating with the final aftershocks of her orgasm. She didn't try to lift her head until his grip loosened, and then she pulled away slowly, careful to clean up all the traces of jizz, catching each string with her tongue. As soon as his cock popped out of her mouth, he took her by the arm and lifted her off the floor, pulling her onto his lap. His tongue invaded her mouth, chasing the taste of his own come, and she happily opened to the attack.

"You should do that more often," he said when he finally lifted his head, and she understood that it wasn't merely a suggestion. She nodded, knowing that she would want to even if he never said anything at all.

The first month of her internship was already over. She only had two more months with Dominic, and she was smart enough to know to make the most of them.

CHAPTER 5

DELICIOUS IN BLACK LEATHER

DOMINIC SURPRISES SONYA *with an invitation to see the summer's hottest band. It's an actual date! Or so she thinks, especially after they fool around in the limo. But when she gets there, she realizes he's not there to see the show, he's there to make deals. When the bassist shows an interest in her, will Dominic protest at all? Or offer her up to his newest client?*

Sonya bought a new dress and Dominic arrived in a long, white limo to pick her up. She had chickenpox on prom night, so this was a completely new experience for her. Dominic was only taking her to a concert, so she didn't want to go overboard with her hair, makeup, and clothes, but she wanted to look good for him, too. She wanted him to be proud to show up with her on his arm, especially since she never, ever expected things to go like this. Their games and flirtation were kept strictly to his office. Never, ever in public. He didn't even act like he knew her most of the time, and now he was picking her up at her house to go to one of the summer's biggest concerts.

She settled on a black miniskirt and a silk sleeveless top.

It was far more risqué than she'd usually wear--in fact; it was the most scandalous thing in her rather conservative wardrobe. He'd certainly never seen her in anything so revealing, but she was feeling bold and sexy. Sonya spent nearly an hour modeling in front of her full-length mirror, checking out all the angles, studying all the details, hoping she wasn't making an ass out of herself by showing off too much of her ass. And yes, her cheeks were a little visible--so was a hint of her black thong. She considered wearing the red one but discarded that idea a little too much. If some-body caught a naughty little glimpse of her panties, that was one thing, but deliberately attracting the eye by wearing red? That was not how she rolled.

Sonya snuck out of the apartment without letting her roommate corner her. She would give her all the details later, but she didn't want to get intercepted and held up answering a million questions. All she wanted to do was get downstairs so Dominic wouldn't have to wait for her--he hated waiting on people. Nothing frazzled his temper more, and Sonya found herself going out of her way to keep his temper intact. He was always so...sweet when he wasn't impatient. Not that she'd ever say that to his face. She had a feeling that he would take offense to being called "sweet"...she also had a feeling that not too many people ever used that word for him before. But sometimes he could be and for whatever reason, those were the times that stood out in her memory the most.

He said he would be at her place at eight, and she timed it perfectly, walking out of the building door just as the limo pulled up. The driver emerged from the white car, crossed to the front, and held the backdoor open for her. She ducked and peered inside before sliding onto the leather upholstery. The short, initial look she had of Dominic stole her breath away. He was always handsome, but she'd never, ever, ever seen him looking so good. He wore black leather pants--leather pants!--and a tight black T-shirt that lovingly hugged his muscled arms and chest. She'd been smashed against that unforgiving chest, been held in place by the unrelenting strength of his arms while he slammed into her, and yet, seeing the cut muscles on such blatant display was enough to make her panties wet.

"Very nice," he murmured as she settled beside him.

"I could say the same thing. I love the leather pants."

He seemed a little uncomfortable at her compliment. Instead of saying anything, he pulled her onto his lap. She squeaked with surprise, but quickly got comfortable on the soft leather, wiggling against the bulge she felt between his legs. He groaned, and she wiggled again, wondering if she could feel the heat of her flesh through his leather. Her silk panties were already soaked through--she might as well not be wearing anything at all. The smell of her arousal mingled with the heady scent of leather, and she was already drowning before he fisted the back of her hair and pulled her into for a demanding--familiar--greeting. Their mouths fused in a hard kiss, and she immediately opened to him, giddy and flushed, aching for more as soon as his tongue slid over hers.

Sonya felt the limo move as the driver put it into gear, but only in a very distant way. All of her senses, her full mental capacity, were focused on Dominic and the heat of his body, the stiffness of his cock against her thigh, the solid deliciousness of his pecs and abs. Her hips moved on their own accord, and she swiveled and rotated, pushing down harder and harder, growing increasingly annoyed by the cage of his zipper. It was only a little thing, something she could have easily done away with, but something always stopped her from taking the upper hand. This time was no different, and she waited--albeit with huge impatience--for him to slip his hand between their bodies and pull down his zipper.

He did slide his hand between them, but he didn't go for the zipper. Instead, he nudged her panties to the side, smiling against her mouth as his fingers came in contact with her silky arousal. He slid the pad of his forefinger up and down her swollen flesh, teasing the labia and spreading the slick fluid until she was a squirming, moaning mess. Why did it feel like years since he last touched her? He'd fucked her over his desk the previous day just before sending her home for the weekend, but that might as well have been a thousand years ago. Her body agreed with that assessment, her clit throbbing with urgency, her heart pounding in her ears with every swipe of his finger, every brush of contact, and hot breath against her lips.

"Do you want more?"

"Yes," she moaned.

"What do you want? This?" He pressed his finger against her swollen clit, letting the flesh throb against his finger, applying more and more pressure without moving, grinding, caressing. It was relentless, and she could only whimper, wordlessly pleading for more. She tried to grind her hips, but he put his hand on her thigh, his strong fingers keeping her perfectly still.

"Horny tonight, aren't you?"

She moaned and nodded, even though she wasn't...hadn't been horny until she saw him. How could anybody look at him and not get horny? She couldn't believe her good luck, and even if he spent the whole drive there tormenting her, torturing her, driving her mad, she would count herself as very, very lucky. If only because she would have the mental image of his leather pants and black T-shirt for the rest of her days.

"Please...I can't..."

"God, I want to fuck you so bad." He kept his forefinger on her clit and slid his middle and ring fingers into her clenching channel, burying them all the way to the final knuckle. He turned his fingers up and tickled her G-spot, pulled his wrist back, and then slammed forward again. She cried out. She couldn't help it. The pleasure went off in colorful rockets through her body, finally bursting in bright red explosions just behind her eyes. She expected him to slap his hand over her mouth to muffle the sounds--like he would if they were in the office--but apparently he didn't care if the driver knew exactly what they were up to. He had no effort to silence her--besides smashing their mouths together again, kissing her as hard as he fingered her.

"Fuck me," she panted out between kisses. He wanted to. Why shouldn't he? His fingers felt amazing, but they weren't enough. They never were. She didn't even enjoy masturbating anymore--every time she tried, all she could think about was how unsatisfying her own hands were. She supposed she should try to find a toy. Somebody somewhere had to make something as satisfying as his big dick. Of course, the best part was what he could do with it, and she didn't think there was a toy in existence that could mimic the pure pleasure of his powerful thrusts as his thighs flexed and his hips slammed forward.

"Can't."

"Why?" She moaned, too far gone to care about whatever his reason might be. He was still moving his fingers with ridiculous force, wrist pumping in and out of her faster and faster.

"Just can't."

Her answering groan let him know exactly what she thought of that stupid excuse. She felt him smile again, and then suddenly the whole world was shifting, and she was flipped backward, her head suddenly below his knees. He folded his arms under her ass, pulling her closer and urging her to wrap her legs around his neck. She giggled a little, though she didn't find anything particularly funny, her heart hammering and her nerves singing. She could feel sweat dripping down the back of her neck, and her long, unbound hair brushed against his biker boots. God, he was killing her...

He closed his mouth around her pussy and sucked her clit between his lips. She gasped. He sucked harder, his teeth holding her tender flesh in place, and then buried his tongue in her wet pussy. He fucked her with his long tongue, slipping in between the buttery flesh while she wiggled and thrust back. He was so strong that he held her in place without any effort, but she couldn't begin to hold herself still. Every thrust and flick of his tongue sent off a series of small explosions, and her limbs were flailing, her spine arching, her mouth opening and closing.

He took his mouth from her pussy long enough to say "Relax" and then she was rolling with it, rolling with him, and the rhythm of his tongue as it rolled in and out of her. Once she stopped resisting him and let the tension melt from her muscles, the wild jerks and flailing stopped, and instead, she was rolling like a boat on the ocean, rising up with the waves and sinking into the troughs without a sound. She closed her eyes against the ceiling of the limo and concentrated on the ribbons of pleasure climbing up her spine and wrapping her entire body in a tighter and tighter package.

He pulled his tongue from her channel and licked up to

her clit, swirling the tip around the raw bundle of her nerves until she went off in a chain reaction that culminated in a long, almost ear-piercing shout. She felt the orgasm from the tips of her toes to the tips of her ears, every inch of her tingling, her blood running hot. He flipped her upright so quickly that he had the whole world spinning around her, and she clasped his shoulders, her small fingers digging into the hard muscles, bracing herself against the tilt-a-whirl feeling. He chuckled--the sound both warm and dark--and then pulled her into another kiss. That did nothing to help her oxygen-starved brain or the sense of blood rushing south, and she could taste her own cum on his tongue and lips. He liked to kiss her after eating her out, and she still wasn't quite used to her own taste, but she was learning to love it. As weird as that seemed to her.

The limo pulled to a stop as he lifted his head from the kiss, and at first, she thought it was only another red light. But he moved her off his lap, depositing her back in the leather seat, and pulled a bottle of mineral water from the bar across from them. He downed it quickly, tossing the bottle as the chauffeur opened the door and offered Sonya his hand. Remembering how she must have sounded, she blushed a deep red as she folded her fingers around his and allowed him to help her out of the car. Dominic was right behind her, wrapping his arm around her waist, and she couldn't help but melt into his embrace, a heady sense of pride suffusing her as they approached the door. There was a line of fans outside waiting to get in --or maybe only waiting for the band to come out of the club--and they all watched with obvious jealousy as Dominic escorted her past security and into the building.

She thought they would go to the club floor--she imagined they must have a table reserved in the VIP section. Did the club have a VIP section? She didn't know for sure, since she'd never been to a concert there before, but she really didn't think Dominic would want to stand in the middle of the crowd all night. He was used to far more consideration than that. But they didn't go to the club floor at all--instead, they went directly to the back of the house where the dressing rooms were. The narrow halls were full of people-- security detail, roadies, and pretty girls--but they all stepped aside as the two of them passed through. Dominic nodded at a few of the men, but he didn't pause to talk to anybody. His strides were long and purposeful, and she practically had to jog in her heels to keep up with him.

They reached the door with the name of the band printed on a plain piece of paper and he tapped his knuckles on the solid wood. A few moments later, it flew open and he was greeted enthusiastically. Sonya felt more than a little out of place as she followed Dominic in, but the feeling was solidified like a punch to the chest when he introduced her. "This is Sonya, my assistant."

Four out of five men nodded at her and then turned their attention back to whatever they were focusing on before, but one of them let his gaze linger. He was holding the bass, his fingers moving over the strings in a distracted, automatic way. She wanted to take a step closer to Dominic, but that didn't seem like a real possibility. Not after that introduction. His assistant? Why would he say that? Wasn't this a date? If this was only a business meeting, why did he tell her to dress up? Why would he pick her up in a limo? Why bring her at all?

A man--he looked like he might be the manager instead of a member of the band--asked her if she needed a pen and paper. Normally, she would have just used her phone to take notes, but she nodded numbly, hurt and surprised and surprised by how much she was actually upset over this. He gave her a half-used pad and a stub of pencil with an apologetic smile, and then she was following Dominic over to the couch. He sat on one end, leaving her no choice but to sit in the middle, between him and the bassist who would not stop staring at her.

Sonya forced herself to pay attention to what the men were saying, but only enough to write down what seemed like the pertinent points. Apparently, they were getting totally fucked over by their current promoter. The contract they signed five years earlier had seemed reasonable at the time, when they were nothing but a bunch of kids from Champagne, Illinois, but now they were poised to hit the scene in a big, big way. Their first album was getting a lot of advanced buzz, and their first single was already getting spun in clubs from coast to coast. Their gigs were getting bigger, attracting more people to larger venues, and they were ready to take the world by storm. Their shitty contract was about to expire, and nobody wanted to sign another one. But they heard so many great things about Dominic from just about everybody they talked to and that was why they sent him tickets--and the car--because they definitely wanted to talk to him while they were in town.

For Dominic's part, he seemed more enthusiastic about the situation than Sonya would have expected. The vast majority of the time, he seemed utterly bored and removed from his job. Like he had no concept of just how fucking awesome it was to work with so many famous, talented, amazing people. Her dad had the same sort of attitude about his job, though his duties brought him into far less contact with genuine celebrities. Sonya hoped she never got that bored with everything. But at the moment, Dominic seemed anything but bored. He leaned forward to listen attentively while the members of the band took turns explaining what they were looking for and answering his questions.

"Curtain's in ten, boys."

"Do you mind hanging out?" The manager asked.

"Of course not."

"Great..."

The bassist stood then. Sonya was aware of the movement, though she didn't let her gaze slide to the left. She'd done a pretty good job of ignoring him completely, keeping her attention focused entirely on Dominic and the meeting. Having never participated in a discussion quite like this, she didn't exactly know what he wanted from her. Why didn't he mention that instead of eating her out? Of course, she appreciated the orgasm, but she would have appreciated some forewarning and maybe a little instruction. Was she supposed to just take stuff like this in stride?

The bassist paused at the manager's shoulder and bent forward, whispering something in his ear. After a moment, he nodded and said, "Now get your head in the game."

The musician smiled easily and slapped the manager on the back before following his bandmates out the door. He was cute. Objectively. She could admit that much. In fact, she wouldn't be surprised if the vast majority of the girls waiting outside the club were there just to see him. He had a good smile, a long, lanky body, soft black hair, and a youthful, angular face. He was probably around her age, but he looked a little younger--especially when he smiled and all that boyish charm was allowed to shine through. But she wasn't impressed. He made her feel like a piece of meat. Sure, she dressed up and showed off a lot of skin, but that was for Dominic's benefit. Not for any jerk who happened to have a dick and a bass guitar.

The manager--what was his name? Had Dominic mentioned it? She quickly flipped through her memory...was it John? That seemed right. Not that it mattered. John gestured for Dominic to lean closer, putting his mouth to Dominic's ear. She had the niggling feeling that they were discussing her. Neither one of them looked over, and there wasn't any concrete evidence of that...but still. Why whisper if they weren't talking about her? And what else would the bassist be whispering about that would require an immediate secret conference with Dominic?

She shifted on the couch, feeling increasingly uncomfortable, the pleasure and heat from the limo fading into a very distant memory. She wanted to go home. She thought about excusing herself for the bathroom and slipping out the door. It would be easy to disappear into the crowd. Then she could use her phone to call for a ride. Or take a cab home--she always brought enough cash with her for a taxi home. Or was she being silly? Letting her imagination run away with her? Assuming the worse?

"We'll be staying until after the show," Dominic announced.

Sonya nodded. She expected as much.

"And Tony would like to see you for a...private show."

John the Manager sniffed at that like he was trying to muffle a laugh. Sonya felt her cheeks coloring again.

"A private show?" She asked slowly.

"Yes. Seems that he thinks you're very pretty." His gaze traveled up and down Sonya's body, and for the first time, she regretted not wearing something that covered her more thoroughly. Like a burka. She almost felt...dirty. Like she'd done something wrong to deserve that sort of look from him. "And he made it a point to request your company."

"But..."

He leveled a look at her that said he wasn't interested in her arguments. She wilted under that look, despite her reservations. A part of her was already trying to justify the situation, trying to rationalize why it was actually a good thing. Tony was cute...right? And plenty of girls would love to be in her position...right? And Dominic definitely wasn't her boyfriend. This wasn't even a date. Hell, she should fuck Tony. She should fuck the entire band. It would serve that bastard right. Who did he think he was? Why did he think he could treat her like a party favor?

Well, she hoped he enjoyed the thought of her fucking everybody who wasn't him. Because after all the bullshit he just put her through--and what he still expected her to do--that was definitely her new game plan. And not just for that night. Dominic Barrows, asshole extraordinaire, was never going to lay another finger on her. And on Monday, not only would she quit her internship, she'd tell her dad everything, and then sue the motherfucker for sexual harassment. Good thing he had deep pockets because she was definitely going to use this little situation against him.

She crossed her arms over her chest, her mind sinking into the comforting red haze of anger as the music started and the bass throbbed through the walls, as distracting and insistent as her furiously beating heart.

CHAPTER 6

WIDE AWAKE

ONCE SONYA DISAPPEARS *with Tony after the show, Dominic realizes his mistake. Unable to admit the truth before, he finally sees that Sonya is more than just a play-thing—she's somebody he doesn't want to lose. But has he realized this in time to stop Tony—or redeem himself?*

John kept talking about important things. Things would have normally held Dominic's full attention. Numbers, projections, marketing, plans for the next single, all sorts of good things. He barely heard one word of it, and *one word* might have been a generous estimation. He tried to realign his attention, tried to drag his focus back to the actual business at hand. *His* business. Business that would be very lucrative to him, if his gut instinct was correct. And his gut was always correct. Poet Metal was going to be huge. They were poised at that sweet spot where talent meant opportunity and he was ready to scoop them up and add them to his stable.

But Dominic wasn't thinking about any of that. He wasn't thinking about the cross-over appeal they had. Wasn't thinking about the contact he had in New York who could probably get them on the shortlist for the upcoming season of Saturday Night Live. Wasn't thinking about the sold-out club and the rowdy fans who demanded three encores before letting the exhausted boys leave the stage for the night. They were all back in their Los Angeles hotel room for the night, each of the young men paired up with at least one beautiful groupie—three in the drummer's case. They were all indifferent to John and Dominic's presence, unmindful of the potential witnesses.

All except the bassist. Who made it a point to pull Sonya into his bedroom suite and close the door as soon as they arrived. An unresisting Sonya. She didn't offer a single argument, didn't try to get out of it, and didn't try to run away. He didn't know if he should be pleased by her obedience or fucking furious that she would allow somebody other than him to touch her. He was leaning towards fucking furious, his heart already beating too fast, his pulse racing, and the back of his neck flushed.

What was that little punk's name? John mentioned it more than once. Maybe Tony? Tony seemed like a good name for that little shitkicker. Who did he think he was, asking for Sonya like that? Especially when he had a varied collection of fans to select from.

Deep down inside, Dominic knew that his anger was not Tony's responsibility. Sure, he asked for Sonya, but who had handed her over? Who had completely ceded her? Who was now waiting for her, unable to leave, unable to think, unable to do anything except imagine her long, glorious legs wrapped around another man? Was he already thrusting into her? Was he already whispering all the dirty things he wanted to do to her? Was she enjoying it? Was she wet for him? Or was she angry?

Would she forgive Dominic?

He wasn't stupid. He saw the look in her eye when Tony pulled her into the adjoining suite.

Get over it. She's just a piece of tail. Not the first and definitely not the last. You had some good times but that doesn't mean anything.

Not the first time he'd given himself that little pep talk. Yeah, she wasn't the first piece of tail, but he had the tendency to grow a little attached to the girls he fucked. Encouraging them to go off with another man was usually a good idea, giving him and the girl in question a little space, a little reality check. *This isn't forever, you don't belong to me, and don't get used to it.*

But this time, the pep talk didn't seem to penetrate his skull. He didn't want the reminders that she wasn't his to keep. This forced him to confront an uncomfortable fact— he wanted to keep her. At least for the time being.

"Dominic? Hey there, buddy, did you hear what I just said?"

Dominic blinked, forcing his attention back to John with an expression of cool interest. Like he'd heard every single word, he just wasn't that impressed with the content. But John wasn't an idiot and he wasn't so dazzled by Dominic—and his status in the entertainment world—to pretend that he was.

"Look, we can talk business later," John started.

Dominic jumped to his feet, suddenly feeling unshackled. The man was absolutely right. That's what his very expensive office was for. He wasn't going to suffer through one more second of the tedious conversation—and of course it wasn't tedious at all. Any other time, he would have been in his element.

"Great. I'll have my secretary call you."

John gave him a curious look. "What has got you so distracted? Is something wrong?"

"No, not at all."

"Was it the show? Look, I know these guys don't appeal to every person...I'm not going to pretend that everybody is going to love them. But they know their demographic. They fit well there."

Dominic brushed John's cajoling aside. He'd heard a little of the music, and it really wasn't bad. They definitely knew their audience well, if the enthusiastic and screaming fans were any indication. Plus, Dominic loved music, regardless of genre. He had a deep respect for talented musicians, especially if they contained that spark of originality, he just happened to want to punch one of the fine musicians in the face.

"It's not that. The show was great. And we'll get the details of the concert worked out."

"Is it that girl?"

Dominic stopped himself from visibly wincing. Was he that obvious? Probably. A bull prancing and stomping around a China shop might have been less obvious. But Tony was probably *inside* her now and...

Sonya cried out. It was definitely her. It was definitely a sound of pleasure, though there was more than a hint of surprise. Like she never expected it to feel *that* good. Dominic couldn't stand still another moment longer. Every protective instinct and possessive inclination he possessed rose up inside of him, pushing him forward, carrying him across the suite to the closed bedroom door.

If the door had been locked, he would have been reduced to banging his helpless fists against the panel until somebody either let him in or called the cops. But the door wasn't locked, neither of them taking the time to put the deadbolt or chain in place, and it opened with a loud bang, slamming against the wall and announcing Dominic's intention to put a stop to the shouts of pleasure.

The sight that greeted him was nearly enough to give him a rage aneurysm. He wasn't angry with her. He had enough self-awareness to realize that this was all, every single second of it, his fault. He was so mad at himself that he could spit nails. Because she was sprawled out on the bed, her clothes were pushed up and yanked aside, in complete disarray. The hot little number she put on just to please him looked like rags, like a mockery of clothes. Her black thong was hooked around one ankle, dangling just above her sexy little shoes, her legs spread and knees akimbo. Her hair was mussed, spread across the pillow behind her, and her lips were swollen and red, looking well-kissed, forming a perfect O of surprise. Tony lifted his head from where it was buried between her thighs, his face flushed, and his mouth shiny and slick.

His roiling emotions must have reached the surface of his face because neither one of them said a word. Tony opened and closed his mouth a few times like he *wanted* to say something, but the silence between the three of them stretched on and on. They were waiting for him to make the first move, to say *something*. This made sense since he was the one who busted up the party like the world's biggest asshole narc.

But his tongue was frozen, his jaw locked in place, jutting and tight. For all the confused fury rolling through him in great, red waves, there was an equally intense, but opposite, sensation. Desire. He wanted Sonya from the moment he saw her. His cock had been leading him around like a willful dog on a leash for weeks now and seeing her like that sent shockwaves directly to his dick.

Finally, his brain clicked into gear, and his mouth began to move, like a piece of ancient and rusty machinery.

"Get up."

The sound of his gravelly order spurred Tony out of his stasis. "Hey men, get the fuck out of here."

Sonya's eyes widened, and she quickly sat up, pulling her top down to cover her tits. "Dominic..."

"Dude. What the fuck is your problem? Get the fuck out of here."

Dominic ignored the young bassist, knowing nothing good could come from a direct confrontation—he didn't want anything to escalate to blows. He just wanted to get Sonya out of that room and into his limo.

"Sonya, come here."

He didn't know what he would do if she flatly refused his order. Pick her up and throw her over his shoulder, fireman style? Repeat himself? He had no doubt fists would fly if she refused to move—Tony would take that to mean he had a leg to stand on. Would probably jump at the chance to defend her and try to throw Dominic out. What Tony probably didn't realize was that Dominic had absolutely no intention of leaving without her. And if he wanted to fight for Sonya, Dominic would go toe to toe until they were both broken-faced and bloody. His blood was running too hot, his tunnel vision stopping him from seeing the reality of the situation. Tony was younger, had thicker muscles, and was probably faster.

But it didn't come to that. Sonya scooted away from Tony and swung her legs over the side of the bed. As soon as she stood, Dominic swooped in, wrapping his arm around her waist and pulling her against them. Her confusion was stamped on her face, and she stared up at him with a question in her eyes. Instead of answering her unspoken inquiry, he lifted her off the floor, swinging her into his arms and cradling her against his chest.

Tony made another effort to demand an explanation, shouting after Dominic as he carried her out of the bedroom. John was standing near the door, looking completely perplexed. Like he had absolutely no idea what was happening or how to explain it or how to even begin to understand it.

"So...?"

"I'll see you in my office on Monday," Dominic bit out.

John nodded. Everybody else in the suite paused what they were doing to watch Dominic march through them, carrying his assistant and looking like he was ready to cut anybody who got in his way. Tony was hot on his heels, wearing nothing but a T-shirt, his naked cock bobbing against his stomach as he shouted after Dominic to bring Sonya back, to face him like a man. Dominic ignored him, ending the confrontation with a sharp slam of the suite door as he stepped into the cool hallway with its sterile, hotel smell. Almost immediately, his head began to clear, each breath quelling his blind, jealous fury.

Sonya didn't speak, and he was thankful for that. She would definitely have questions, primarily, *what the fuck was that all about?* And Dominic didn't have an answer for her. Not a verbal one, anyway. Maybe he could provide all the explanation without ever actually saying a word. All he really knew was that it felt good, *right*, to have her within his arms, to feel her heat soak through his shirt, to sense her breath on his neck.

John must have called down to the valet station because his limo was waiting for him, the chauffeur standing with the door open. Dominic acknowledged him with a flick of his eyes before sliding into the backseat, still clutching Sonya like an ill-gotten treasure.

"Dominic..."

Fear of the question he heard in her voice, fear of trying to find an answer, and anger at the genuine fear he felt, drove him forward, drove him to silence her before she asked him a question he couldn't ignore. He claimed her mouth and this time, he didn't hold any part of himself away from the kiss. He wasn't thinking clearly. But maybe for the first time, he was thinking *right*.

For the first time, he was thinking about her as somebody he might lose, not a toy he could so casually toss away.

For the first time, he wasn't pretending that she was just scratching an itch anybody could reach.

For the first time, the kiss was tinged with something bittersweet, as his long-suppressed guilt for being obsessed with a colleague's daughter finally reached up from the depths of his subconscious. He'd first met Sonya when she wasn't quite eighteen, the bright, beautiful daughter of the first man to join his agency after five years of Dominic building it on his own. She'd been a senior in high school, the head of her class, beautiful and stunning in every way. That dinner had been excruciatingly long as Dominic struggled with physical reactions he couldn't control—physical reactions he never expected. Why would her laugh make him hard? And why, when their hands briefly touched as they both reached for the basket of bread, did his stomach flip and flop and flutter like the first time he saw a naked breast?

He kept his distance, hoping his lustful feelings would fade, feeling his ardor lessen as she became more of a distant memory. It wasn't long before he convinced himself he never wanted her at all, or at least the first pull of desire had been a fluke. He added to that a forced layer of indifference, a shield of pure ice that refracted the truth, twisting it into something he could live with. Something as cold and indifferent as to the walls he'd put up in defense.

And all of that was in his kiss, in the movement of his mouth and the hungry, almost desperate way he claimed her lips, drinking her all in. He didn't think about the way Tony must have kissed her, or wonder if the faint breeze of alcohol on her breath was from her drink or the bassist's mouth. He held her close, his fingers sinking into her flesh with just enough force to remind her that he was not going to let her go. Her heart was pounding against her ribs—he could feel the insistent thump echoing through his own chest, and her breath came in short, heated gasps.

His cock throbbed with equal intensity, and the leather pants no longer seemed like a great idea. He'd been aching for her since he first touched her, and when he'd been drinking her sweet cum straight from her pussy, he thought he would actually burst through his pants, his cock feeling thick and hard as a brick. Maybe he should have fucked her on the way to the meeting, claiming her with such complete intensity that it would mark her as his, keeping all other would-be suitors at bay.

Yes, in hindsight, that would have been a much better route to take. What had he been thinking by keeping his dick in his pants?

But he wasn't going to whip it out now, either. Not quite. He didn't want to just have a quickie in the back of the car—he wanted to prove a point. Whether that was to Sonya or to him, he couldn't quite say. And what, exactly, he needed to prove, he couldn't quite say, either. But he kept his mouth fused to hers, and his hands rubbed over her shoulders and down her back, then circled back over her ribs so he could cup the sweet weight of her tits in his large palms.

The smell of her desire and his sweat and leather filled the backseat, spiced by her perfume and the waft of shampoo every time he moved his fingers through her hair. She matched his intensity, kiss for kiss, but he sensed something darker in her caress. He could almost taste the coppery tinge of her anger, the electric current racing under her skin. He would accept that anger, absorb it if he had to, or weather it if she wanted to unleash herself. She had more than a right to her anger, and he didn't really believe he could simply kiss it out of her, smother it with his passion until she forgot that he'd hardened his heart against her.

The limo pulled to a stop and he heard the gentle ping of the driver's door opening, alerting him to the fact that they'd reached his building. The gap between the car and his apartment door seemed insurmountable, but he had enough of his self-control remaining to get her to his front door without completely ravishing her. He hoped.

He assisted her out of the limo with a hand on her elbow, tightening his hold as they approached the lobby doors, practically dragging her into the building. She struggled to keep up with his long, urgent strides, until she stumbled into the elevator behind him, falling into his chest and driving him back against the wall. With her so close, his arms automatically closed around her, but this time she was the one who made the first move, pressing her mouth to his as the elevator doors closed behind them, her hands spreading across his hard pecs. She held him against the wall, the tiny cabin racing up the sky-scraper he called a home, exploring his mouth with surprising boldness.

When the elevator dinged their arrival on the twenty-fifth floor, he lifted her, wrapping her legs around his waist.

She held on with all her strength, grinding her pussy down onto his bulge, making it rather difficult for him to walk. The pressure in his balls was the worst, his leather pants so tight they felt like they might cut his circulation. Tingles traveled up and down his leg, and his muscles were tight, bunched up in his thighs and ass.

It took some doing, but he got his apartment unlocked and opened, the motion-sensor lights flipping on as soon as he crossed the threshold. Sonya lifted her head then and looked around, her eyes wide beneath her tousled hair, a soft *wow* escaping as she took in her new surroundings, a rather pointed reminder that she'd never been invited back to his home. Though really, it was only the place he slept a few times a week. His office was more of a home than his apartment had ever been.

He carried her into the bedroom, the final steps the most painful and awkward of all. Once he deposited her on the bed, he immediately set about removing her clothes, and as he pulled her skirt off he noticed something he hadn't seen before. A bite mark on her thigh. It wasn't dark—it might even fade by the next morning—but it definitely wasn't courtesy of him. He reached out to touch it, the tips of his fingers gently brushing over the purple shape. She shuddered in response, her entire body quivering, her legs parting ever so slightly. He felt the ever so slight indent of teeth, and something inside seemed to break apart—or maybe it snapped back into place like a long dislocated knee finally set right.

"I'm sorry," Dominic whispered, the words harsh like they had to be torn free from his throat.

She caught her breath, her chest hitching ever so slightly as each syllable sank into her skin. He kissed a path around the purple skin, hoping she understood how much he was apologizing. He caught the skin between his lips, sucking on it gently, drawing blood near to the surface, obscuring the physical reminder of Tony—of Dominic's nearly catastrophic mistake. He lifted his head to admire his work, catching a powerful whiff of her arousal, instantly making his mouth water with painful anticipation.

He pulled himself away from her inner thigh, kissing his way up her body and then sitting back on his heels, surveying the situation. There was one thing missing—one thing he needed to do if he was going to fuck her like he longed to. He backed off from the bed and unzipped his pants, finally giving his dick a hint of relief. The insistent throbbing wouldn't fade until he was finally buried inside of her, but at least the most pointed of the pain had faded away.

He quickly rid himself of all his clothes, crossing to his dresser to grab his condoms and the handcuffs with long chains between the cuffs. He snapped the cool steel around her right wrist and then ran his hand under her leg, hooking her behind the knee and lifting her leg. He snapped the other bracelet around her ankle and did the same on her left side, opening her wide to his hands and eyes and hunger.

"Comfortable?"

She nodded, her eyes locked on him, her skin gleaming with sweat. He took the condom from its wrapper and slid it down his shaft, covering his dark red shaft and his swollen mushroom head. He gripped her ankles, just below the bracelets, and then slid his palms over her smooth skin, along the lovely curves of her calves and knees, the slight widening of her thighs, his thumbs sliding along the seams between her swollen pussy and her thighs.

Dominic fingered her pussy, collecting the slick, sweet juice from her opening and spreading it over the condom.

He helped himself to her arousal, returning to that tantalizing heat, rubbing her with gentle fingers, more tenderly than he'd ever touched her before. She mewed with delight, making tiny, sweet sounds under her breath every time he slid his long finger in and out of her body. She lifted and pivoted her hips, though she couldn't move as much as she wanted to, with her ankles locked to her wrists.

He pulled her pink folds apart so he could admire her whole pussy, dipping his head down to lap at her clit. The bundle jerked under his tongue, her pulse instantly jumping, throbbing against his tongue. He teased it like he knew she liked, with just the tip of his tongue swirling and dancing over her hot skin. She was growing hotter by the second, her soft sounds turning into longer, louder moans, her body vibrating with the force of her pleasure.

"Please," she gasped out. "Need you, Dominic. Don't want to wait anymore."

The sentiment was convincing enough, but it was the sound of her quivering voice, the gentle plea behind each word, the unexpected, ragged emotion underlying each word that made him lift his head. He stretched her legs as wide as he could and angled his cock towards her slick channel, pushing his hips to sink down into the achingly vibrant, impossibly rich heat. It overpowered him completely, shackling him in chains that felt just as real as the handcuffs holding her in place. He kept moving until he bottomed out, his balls brushing against her ass. He brought her ankles together and pushed them back, until her toes were touching the wall above her head, forcing her body to squeeze even tighter around his shaft.

There was nothing to hold him back. Nothing to stop him from drilling down into her depths with all the energy and fury, lust and passion, desire and guilt that he'd been trying, and failing, to fight for four years. Their flesh slapped together, his balls bouncing off her ass with every powerful thrust. He moved his hands from her ankles, but she didn't let her legs drop, keeping her toes braced against the wall while he returned his attention to her tits. Her nipples were hard and pointed the pink flesh as pretty as twin pink roses.

He fucked her like that until his mouth tingled and he felt the prick of desire for something more. Widening her legs, slightly adjusting himself against her, he leaned down to find her mouth once again. But before he claimed it, he whispered the words he'd long felt, had wanted to declare more than once, syllables constantly dancing on the tip of his tongue, waiting for the perfect moment to escape.

"You're mine." A promise. A declaration. Even a warning, if she wanted to hear it that way. But the complete and utter truth. She was his. It didn't matter what anybody thought about that or what anybody said. He himself wasn't even fully aware of all the implications of it. But he wouldn't take it back, wouldn't let her pretend she didn't hear or couldn't understand.

"You're mine," he repeated, punctuating the simple phrase with a hard, powerful thrust. She nodded her head, but that wasn't enough for him. He wanted to hear her say it, too. Wanted her to complete the pact and echo his promise.

"Say it." His voice held more encouragement than cold demand, and more of a plea than he would have liked. If she was listening—if she was paying attention—she would have a whole new world of understanding about what was happening between them. Or maybe not...maybe she was too inexperienced and naïve to understand that he'd just lay his heart on the line, putting it out in the open for anybody to trample over.

She didn't make him wait for a response, though. She saved him from the agony, kept moving her body against his, and snapping her hips with equal intensity. "I'm yours. I'm yours, Dominic. Don't ever do that...don't ever treat me like that again."

"I won't," he rasped. "Never, ever again."

"I didn't want to be with him."

"I know that."

"I want to be with you."

"You are with me," he assured her, his lips gliding over hers between each word. She moaned and moved to hold him, just enough to give in the handcuffs to allow her to wrap her arms and legs around him. She held on tight to him for the rest of the night, her taut muscles flexing around him, her body full of unknown strength, more than capable of drawing him back into her again and again. He wanted to fuck her all night, and the minutes melted away as quickly as seconds, each hard drive sending her closer to the peak of her pleasure—and sending him to the breaking point where he feared he'd lose the last of his control.

When he felt himself nearing the point of no return, he made the decision to pull out of her body—an act that was almost agonizing. And yet, it was for a good reason. He gripped his shaft and began stroking himself, catching the condom and pulling it away without missing a beat. He kneeled over her, aiming his cock at her chest and stroking furiously while his other hand massaged her pussy, gently grinding his fingers into her clit. He coaxed the fires that were already burning, fanning the flames inside her body until he felt the tell-tale tension and heard the difference in her moans.

"Inside," she gasped. "Touch me inside…I need…"

He pushed two fingers into her pussy and curled the tips, massaging her G-spot before she could finish articulating her request. It was like pushing the button on a detonator. She immediately went off, and the sight—let alone the sound and the smell and the *feel* of her pleasure—was more than enough to set him off, too. Long white strings of cum burst from him, painting her stomach, some strands hanging from her full tits, sliding over her skin with her slick sweat.

Dominic held himself together long enough to free her feet and wrists from the bracelets, then collapsed against her, his arms wrapped around her like he feared she might escape.

CHAPTER 7

I KNEW YOU WERE TROUBLE

SONYA SAT STRAIGHT UP in bed, her heart hammering so loudly she couldn't hear anything else, sleep still blurring her vision, confusing her further. Something had pulled her from a deep sleep, rousing her in a strange room and a strange bed. Her attention leaped from object to object, taking in the unfamiliar details surrounding her. She didn't recognize any of it, the faces in the picture frame complete strangers, the decor created by an unknown hand. Sunlight streamed through the window, the floor-to-ceiling panes covered by gauzy curtains that rippled in the cool air blowing from the vents in the floor below.

A light touch at the small of her back pulled her eyes to the left, and her confusion melted away, the pieces falling into place. Dominic had brought her home the night before, carrying her straight to his bed and making love to her again and again until she passed out from pure exhaustion. Her skin was flaky and itchy from the dried sweat and other fluids, and the room still smelled vaguely of their passion. His eyes were closed, but she could tell he was awake. She moved to slip away, thinking she could freshen up, but he moved faster, putting his hand on her thigh and holding her in place.

"Where do you think you're going?"

"To brush my teeth."

He shook his head, his heavy palm moving up her leg, over her hip, and up her chest. He gently pushed her back to the thick feather pillows, his arm immediately curving around her and pulling her in close. She sighed softly, all thoughts of escaping evaporating completely. Her eyes felt heavy, her heart beating slowing until she hovered between awake and asleep, only aware of the heat of his body against her back and the gentle warmth of the sun reaching through the window.

How could this be anything but a dream? When she woke up next, she'd be alone, in her own bed. Or worse yet, a strange hotel bed, with her clothes strewn from one end of the suite to the other. How could Dominic be holding her so close? How could she be waking up in his bed? Sonya never even fantasized about what it would be like to be literally taken to his bed--that always seemed far too personal for him.

Sleep tried to pull her back down into oblivion, but she resisted the heavy feeling in her eyelids and limbs. His cologne danced around her head and settled inside her nostrils, filling her with his spicy scent, and she felt safe. Safer than she could ever remember feeling before. The thought almost made her laugh. Safe with Dominic? The man who seemed happy to give her away like she was a cheap whore? The man who always took what he wanted from her? The man who shook the very foundations of her life, making her insecure in ways she never even imagined? That was the man who made her feel as safe and content as a pampered kitten?

Everything that happened to her after Dominic picked her up seemed like a dream--and some parts were more like a nightmare. She could still smell Tony's sweat and sour breath, still feel his callused fingers pulling at her clothes, roughly groping at her breasts, and wiggling between her thighs like inelegant snakes. She'd been determined to see it through, to flaunt her sexual power and feed off of Tony's energy to make Dominic pay, but in hindsight, she was very grateful that she didn't ultimately have to go through with it. How could she look at herself in the mirror if she had? How could she even stand to live with herself?

How could she stand to look at Dominic, for that matter? Did she really like the way he made her feel? Did she love to be treated like crap? Yes, he stopped her before she had any real regrets, but that hardly made him some sort of hero. She should let the whole experience be a lesson. She'd leave the internship early; she'd travel for a few weeks before her fall semester started. She'd find herself a new lover, and if she ever thought about Dominic at all, it would only be with a vague sense of nostalgia...

He shifted slightly, disturbing the pillow and refreshing the smell of his cologne and sweat. Her senses were immediately on high alert, her stomach flip-flopping, a sense of satisfaction washing over her, thanks to the pheromones saturating her brain, triggering the release of all kinds of hormones. Almost as soon as her plan to escape presented itself, it dissipated, leaving her happily trapped in the cage created by his arms. Thoughts of Tony dissipated, too. He didn't matter. Dominic was the only one who mattered.

She was trapped in more ways than just one. It wasn't just his superior strength and his solid arms holding her in place. What was she going to do? God, how was she ever going to figure things out? How was she ever going to make sense of her feelings?

"You're thinking too loud. I'm trying to sleep."

Sonya frowned. "How can I think too loud?"

"I don't know, but you're keeping me awake."

He lifted himself from the bed and flipped her around like she was nothing but a doll in his arms. He stared down at her and her heart wiggled and flipped, like a little puppy dog pleased to finally have her master's attention. His dark eyes pierced her, staring through her like he could read her thoughts if he looked hard enough. She nearly squirmed from the intensity of his stare, fighting the urge to look away. When he finally moved, she expected demanding pressure as their mouths connected, but the kiss was so delicate that it whisked the breath right from her lungs. She felt a pull through her chest like he was literally drawing the oxygen from her and then sweet, simple warmth flooded her on his exhale.

There was no rush, and she had time to linger over every second and nuance of his lips. When his tongue swept past her lips, she did regret not escaping to the bathroom, but it was a brief thought--the slight wiggle of his tongue ignited every nerve-ending along her spine, distracting her from everything but the sense of pleasure growing by the second.

She wrapped her arms around him, her fingers teasing the back of his neck, along his hairline, over the sensitive skin normally covered by his collar.

He drifted from her mouth, his lips traveling over her cheekbones, her eyelids, her brow, each moment of contact as light and soft as a butterfly wing. She turned her face, pressing her mouth against his throat and shutting her eyes against the battery of emotions suddenly assaulting her.

God, she shouldn't let him do this to her. Wasn't she strong enough to resist him? Why did her body and her heart have to work in perfect harmony against her common sense? He intoxicated her, he left her shaking, he worked her over and made her ache, and he could turn her whole world inside out and upside down with nothing more than the pressure of his lips.

When he finally lifted his head, she was dazed and flushed, her lips tingling and sparking. She ran her tongue over her bottom lip, her gaze caught in his. He looked different in the early morning sunlight, unlike anything she'd ever seen. The night before, he'd been a predator, sleek and dangerous, ready to her heart, her soul, her body, ready to destroy anybody who got in his way. But now he looked rumpled and sweet, more like a lion cub than the king of a jungle. She ran her fingers through his hair, tousling it even more, and the corners of her mouth lifting in a smile she couldn't stop.

"There. Did that help?"

Sonya blinked up at him, her mind a muddle, too confused to understand what he was asking. He must have seen the confusion in her eyes because he chuckled softly, the sound more good-natured, warmer, than anything she'd ever heard from him. She immediately wanted to bottle it, whisk it away to some secret closet where she could enjoy it again and again.

"I think it did. Your thoughts have quieted down a bit. Haven't they?"

"Oh. Yeah." She nodded. "I guess so."

He touched the side of her face with the back of his hand, gently caressing her cheek before dipping his head to kiss the corner of her mouth. Even that slight moment of contact sent a chill down her spine. She wiggled her hips, shifting her weight on the bed, her legs automatically falling open to accommodate him.

"You guess so? You should go back to sleep. Nobody should be up this early on a Sunday morning."

She turned her head, smirking a bit when she saw the time. "It's already after nine. We're well on our way to being lazy bums."

"Nope. Not on Sunday mornings. On Sunday mornings, we are perfectly within our rights to stay in bed until noon."

"Is that a fact?"

"Yes, ma'am."

"I've never seen this side of you before."

"What side?"

"The lazy bum side," she murmured, curling her legs around his hips. If he wanted to stay in bed, she wasn't going to argue with him. She lifted herself up, pressing her throbbing flesh against his growing cock. She moved her hips, grinding against him until he was fully hard, and his long, thick shaft like a steel pipe pressing into her thigh.

"You seem to like it."

"It's quite attractive." She was so wet she knew it would be easy to adjust herself and have him glide right inside. The thought itself was enough to awaken her entire body, making her tingle from head to her toes. Higher-order thoughts began to shut down, one by one, leaving her with nothing but pure hunger and instincts to guide her. Her senses were busy with the job of absorbing him, detail by detail until he was inside of her body, mind, and heart.

It was even easier than she expected to bring him inside of her. Their lips locked once again, but this time with more intensity and heat, and when he slipped inside, it felt very much like a piece was being returned to her body. He filled her completely, his balls resting against her skin, his body holding her down to the mattress, making her ache for more. She tried to look at him when he broke away from the kiss, but the sight of him, rumpled and sweet and overwhelming, was too much for her to withstand. She had to close her eyes, lifting her chin slightly and dropping her head back as he eased away, and then surged forward, like the ocean pulsating and pounding against the welcoming shore. She was an inlet, a perfectly formed and protected bay, offering him safe harbor every time he pushed into her.

It was funny how well she knew him now, how much she could anticipate. Funnier still, how much she didn't know. How much he surprised her. How little she could ever anticipate what he would do, what he wanted from her, how he would react, how he would even beg in his own, subtle way.

God, she was falling for him. If she hadn't already plummeted to the bottom of the deep pit, impaling her heart on some ragged, sharp stick, jutting out from the darkness, unseen and unknown until it was far too late. Her heart still beats as strongly as before and that's why she couldn't tell if she was still falling or if she'd already been pierced. Maybe she was only addicted to him. Maybe she was addicted to the rush, to having the forbidden, to living a secret, a lie. Maybe she liked that she had to keep it from her father, from her colleagues, from everybody because the secret bound her to him.

Whatever was going on between them, he felt it too. She believed that. After his little display the night before, how could she possibly believe anything else? How could she possibly say anything else? They were locked together now, entwined physically and emotionally, and after the night they shared, how could she resist that? He already knew her, but now he had a free pass to access all the secrets--she wasn't going to be able to deny him anything ever again. She had absolutely no desire to do so. She just wanted to surrender to him, and it was that small act, that almost impossible admission that made her heart beat faster and her blood pump hotter through her veins.

He rolled onto his back, bringing her with him, and positioning her over his body. The new angle drove his cock deep inside of her, and even the discomfort she felt when he nudged her back wall couldn't make her stop moving. His hands traveled down her spine to cup her ass, his fingers squeezing the flesh, urging her down on top of him with sharper, harder pushes until they established an almost brutal rhythm, short and staccato. When he had her moving just the way he wanted her to move, he began caressing her, sliding his fingertips up and down the crack of her cheeks. Before long, the tip of one was resting on her pucker, pressing playfully against her little rosebud.

She shifted backward, arching her back as she felt the pressure of his blunt finger against her flesh. After only a moment of effort, she felt the heat of his skin broaching the opening, sinking in deeper and deeper. The foreign pressure and unexpected friction made her freeze, but he wasn't going to be dissuaded. He pushed deeper until his entire finger was buried in her ass, and when he wiggled it, sparks of fire shot up her spine and flooded her throat. She couldn't even speak, but she did manage to make a sound that could only be interpreted as pure pleasure, as the shapeless request for more.

He worked his finger in and out of her, using the same rhythm as his hips so he was always filling her. Once the expected burn faded away, she relaxed more, making it even easier for him to fuck her ass. He gradually added a second finger, stretching out her flesh, coaxing her into accepting the slight pain before it was buried under swelling waves of pleasure. It took her less time to get used to the second finger-probably because she was distracted by the goal of bringing her body down on his dick in just the right way, finding just the right angle to hit her G-spot and send her spiraling even deeper into the ocean of bliss she found herself surrounded by.

By the time he added a third finger, she realized what his end-game was. Usually, she didn't really like the thought of anal sex, and she didn't especially see the point of it, but the way three fingers felt inside of her made her ache to know what his dick could do. She'd never experienced anything so intense, and she didn't know if she wanted to get away from his fingers or push back even harder, if she could speak or if she should just scream her pleasure as it built and built and built. It almost seemed like too much to take, like it would be safer for her to simply beg him to stop, to roll away from his body and pant and gasp until she caught her breath once again. But he wasn't going to let her roll away and really? Did she even want to?

No, she wanted to be taken to the very peak, the very top of the mountain. She wanted to go to the highest point possible, and if the only way to get there was to sink down on his thick cock, letting the pulsing flesh fill her ass, stretching her and push her and make her ache and burn in new, impossible ways, then that's what she would do. She couldn't do anything less than follow him down whatever road he wanted to lead her on.

After what felt like an eternity, he pulled his fingers free from her body and reached for his nightstand. Without missing a beat he poured lube from a small bottle onto all three fingers and returned them to her warm, welcoming flesh. With the oil, it was much easier to ease them inside, and she didn't even feel a twinge of pain as he stretched her once again. In fact, she realized at that moment how divine it would feel to have another cock slipping inside, thrusting into her, rubbing against Dominic's shaft through the thin, almost non-existent membrane of her skin. Maybe someday she'd suggest it--in the far distant future. She wasn't sure Dominic would be into sharing her, especially after his reaction to Tony the night before.

A reaction that seemed all the more intense now that her body was in such an aroused, stimulated state. She shouldn't allow herself false hope but maybe....maybe it meant something.

His fingers disappeared once again and he held her by the hips, lifting her up until his dick slipped from her slick channel. She realized what he meant to do and opened her mouth to protest, suddenly certain that she was in no way capable of taking his full girth inside her barely stretched hole. His blunt tip pressed against the stretched skin, demanding an entrance despite the natural, physical resistance. He pulled her chest down to his, his mouth teasing hers with the briefest contact before he whispered, "Relax, sweetheart. This will work; you just need to trust me."

Trust. That was the problem, wasn't it? She could love him, and she probably did. She could lust for him day and night and even surrender herself to that lust, turning her body over completely to pleasure, to satisfaction. But trust him? Completely? Wasn't that just asking for trouble? And wasn't she supposed to be smarter than that? Well, maybe not. She hadn't done much to demonstrate her awesome intelligence lately. But it was already too late to put up any resistance. It was easier to just relax, to let him lift his hips and push until he was past the barrier and had nothing to stop him from sliding in deeper and deeper until he had nowhere else to go and she was fully seated on his cock.

"Breathe," he repeated, again and again, a gentle but necessary reminder as she started to gasp for oxygen. Breathe, breathe, breathe in and breathe out, over and over and over until the pain started to feel good until the pure physical assault turned into a caress. She shifted to try to relieve the pressure, but that did little to no good, every small movement enough to create enough friction and heat to light a Christmas party. She took his free hand in hers, entwining their fingers, gripping with all of her strength as she experimentally wiggled her hips. Then it was a brief up and down. Then she grinded herself in a tight circle, working him even deeper. Every subtle difference was like a fresh batch of fireworks going off beneath her skin, the lights and sounds and heat and smell of each gigantic boom driving her forward, making her yearn for more.

That was why she didn't hear the door, why she wasn't aware of their audience. She was chasing down something elusive, but something finally within her grasp, staring at Dominic's beautiful face, his eyelashes fanning across his cheeks, his mouth twisted in a silent but unmistakable moan of pleasure.

Fiona's unmistakable gasp of horror was as loud as a gunshot. Sonya's stomach flipped painfully, and she closed her eyes as a familiar sense of humiliation washed through her. She knew how this was going to play out. She knew Dominic would say something cruel, something to show both Fiona and Sonya exactly how little she meant to him. She couldn't go through that. Not after the night they had. Not in front of the queen bitch herself, a woman who had even more reason to cut Sonya down as quickly and effectively as they could.

She'd say this was Sonya's doing. Sonya's fault. And maybe she'd be right. But she wasn't going to withstand a barrage from King Dickhead and his beloved Queen. She rolled away from him, jumping to her feet and grasping for the sheet as Fiona's eyes narrowed to slits. Sonya could practically see the hair go up on the back of her neck, and if she'd been a cat, her tail would have been puffed three times fuller.

Fiona didn't say a word, but she didn't have to. Sonya read her loud and clear. She wasn't going to wait for Dominic to find his voice. Fiona's death glare melted into a treacly smile.

"Jesus Christ, Dom. Did you really need to squeeze one more in before we shared the big news?" She turned her body to the side and ran her hand over her stomach, which had the slightest of bumps.

CHAPTER 8

LOCKED OUT OF HEAVEN

SONYA'S HEART jumped to her throat, her stomach twisting violently. Fiona was pregnant? Fiona was pregnant and Dominic *knew*? Sonya had to get out of there before she puked.

Sonya gathered her clothes with as much dignity as she could muster, the heat of Fiona's furious gaze singing Sonya's skin and burning a hole right through her. For the first time, Dominic was utterly silent, and maybe just as helpless as Sonya beneath Fiona's withering glare. He certainly didn't seem interested in helping her. What was he going to do? Make another grand gesture? Wait until Fiona went away and then reassures her that she meant something to him? Or maybe he'd just fire her, the final humiliation, and be rid of her forever.

If Dominic didn't fire her, she would have to quit. Because this had to stop. It had to. God, she deserved so much better than this, than him. For a few brief moments, they were beautiful together and Sonya had let herself believe that maybe...oh, she'd let herself believe so many ridiculous things. She supposed that was the power of self-delusion when it came to really great sex and a man who was physical perfection, even if he seemed to be an emotional mess with the maturity level of an eighteen-year-old frat pledge.

Fiona waited until Sonya pulled on her ridiculous little dress, wearing the most obnoxious smirk Sonya ever saw.

"Oh, look at that pouty little face. Did you think you were special, sweetheart? Oh, I bet you did."

Sonya closed her eyes and waited for Dominic's confirmation. She didn't expect anything but agreement from him. Why should she? Fiona was perfect for him, for his life, for his position. She was beautiful, sophisticated, and worldly, and Sonya felt like nothing more than a child in comparison.

"Just get out of my way," Sonya said between gritted teeth.

"Oh no, you don't get to take that attitude with me, little girl. You don't get to act like the wronged party when you're the little slut sleeping with *my* fiance. The father of *my* child. And you can't even plead ignorance, can you? You tried to steal my man, and you knew what you were doing the whole time."

Sonya didn't want to be having this conversation at all, much less not while her body was still tingling from Dominic's touch and her clothes were in a pathetic bundle in her arms. Fiona's glare flew over Sonya's head to land on Dominic, and she very much felt like a bone caught between two snarling, junkyard dogs, too hungry and angry to walk away. The tension in the room was already high, but it seemed to go up another level.

"I wasn't trying to steal anybody, I..."

"Oh shut up. Nobody cares about your lies. I know your type. Hell, I *was* your type. And if you were going after anybody else, I'd probably applaud you. A girl's got to do what she's got to do, but not with *my* man. Do you understand me?"

Sonya's head swiveled to Dominic, her eyes wide and questioning. Was he really going to allow that woman to talk to her that way? To tell her to *shut up* like she was a wayward child? Oh, he was? Sonya took a deep breath. Fine. Fine. She was tired of this and if she was going to lose her job and her self-respect, at least she'd go down fighting.

"Maybe if you were half the woman you think you are, he wouldn't be spending time with me. You must be a...a real cold fish in bed if he keeps coming after me. Because I gotta tell you, as much as we fuck, I was assuming you two were waiting until after you were married."

Fiona's eyes widened, and for the first time, Sonya felt something like power. She didn't want to get in a fight with Fiona over Dominic. She didn't want to fight anybody. She didn't want to expose herself, didn't want either of them to know just how much she felt for him. But she was tired of being kicked in her exposed belly. Tired of being treated like garbage. Dominic wasn't even *nice* to her. There were plenty of good-looking men in Los Angeles, and she was sure that Dominic was not the only one with a great cock and decent skills. Dominic wasn't the only man alive who could make her heart beat faster.

This had to end.

Sonya missed the way Fiona's fingers wiggled, the sudden clenching of her left hand, or else she might have simply shoved her way past the other woman and continued out the door. But she missed the little signals, and her anger was building by the second. Dominic was the author of this entire clusterfuck, and this bitch had the nerve to stand there at and yell at *her*? Just twelve hours earlier, some asshole was pawing at Sonya's body like she was a prize he won at the fair, and Dominic had just handed her over. Waking up beside him had temporarily masked that humiliation, but now the mask was ripped away, and *everything* was allowed to surface.

"You know he fucked me right after we met the first time? Did you ever hear a weird catch in his voice on one of your endlessly boring calls? The only way he could get through that tedious bullshit was with me on my knees beneath his desk. Did you ever wonder why he worked late every single night? Or are you so naïve you really thought that he had contracts to go over?"

Fiona's eyes narrowed. "I told you to shut up."

"Well, I'm telling you to go fuck yourself. You better get used to it if you're going to marry Dominic because near as I can tell, the last thing he wants to do is put his dick inside of you."

Fiona reacted faster than Sonya could blink, slapping her across the face so quickly that Sonya never even saw her hand move. Surprising heat stung her red cheek, and her eyes tingled with a mixture of pain and anger. For a hanging moment, all three of them were perfectly still, and the room was silent except for the memory of skin connecting with skin. Sonya slowly raised her fingers to her cheek, tenderly touching the hand-shaped mark. It didn't really hurt once the initial sting faded, but it pushed Sonya right over the edge.

Most people thought of her as a girly girl, but there was a reason she could keep up with Dominic, matching him stroke for stroke, staying with him every second as he used his muscles to pound into her body. She'd been on the varsity soccer and volleyball teams in high school, and she stayed active afterward, running and lifting weights. She was deceptively small, her strength obscured by her petite stature. Fiona had at least four inches on her, with slightly broader shoulders and maybe extra ten or fifteen pounds. She may have thought she had every advantage. Or maybe she was just a bitch with poor impulse control because, in spite of making the first move, she was caught completely unawares when Sonya launched herself at the older woman.

She buried one hand in her hair, gripping the silky strands and winding the whole handful around her fingers. She closed the other hand in a fist, far beyond thinking clearly. She cocked her arm back, ready to let fly and release all her anger and embarrassment, fueling the blow with every second that Dominic ever treated her like a jerk, every second of doubt and insecurity, every second of self-loathing because goddamnit she let it happen *again*.

That punch was never delivered—much to Fiona's benefit. Had Sonya been allowed to let fly, she probably would have broken Fiona's perfect little nose and blackened both her beautifully made-up eyes. Dominic caught Sonya's fist in his palm and yanked her back, pulling her out of striking distance and putting his body between the two angry women.

"Stop it. Both of you."

"Why did you stop her? Let her punch me if it makes her feel better. Let her punch a pregnant woman. I'll have her ass in jail so fast...not to mention the lawsuit for all my hospital bills and pain and suffering. I wouldn't mind owning a little bitch for the rest of her miserable life."

Sonya's stomach lurch as she realized what Dominic

had saved her from. There was no way to punch a pregnant woman and have a defense. Even if, for just a moment, she forgot Fiona was pregnant. The nausea returned, and she lurched away from Dominic. She had to get out of there before things got even worse. She shouldered her way past Fiona, surprised when the woman let her walk past without a word. She would have really liked to get dressed—going out in public in nothing more than a tiny bra, a thong, and her jacket didn't seem like the best idea, but she could not stay in that apartment for one more second. She would just get dressed in the elevator.

"Sonya, wait." Dominic's voice was unusually tight, but it lacked the usual note of command.

"No."

"Sonya. I need to talk to you."

She yanked the front door open and looked over her shoulder. "Fuck you. Fuck *you* and fuck you. Also, I quit."

Sonya marched through the door and slammed it behind her as hard as she could, rattling the whole wall. She thought she heard the crashing of a frame on the hardwood floor. Good. She wished she had the chance to destroy a few more things. Something about the shattering glass assuaged a little of her anger, but her vision was still blurry and everything still felt too hot. By the time the elevator dinged open, she realized she was crying and forced herself to take a breath. She waited for the click of Dominic's door, but it never opened. He wasn't going to come after her.

That's a good thing. That means he actually got my message. And I'll never, ever have to see him again.

She stepped into the elevator, not looking around again as the doors swished shut behind her. She mechanically pulled her dress back on and cinched her jacket as tight as she could, still feeling completely naked and utterly vulnerable and suddenly very, very tired. By the time the doors opened to the lobby of Dominic's building, all the fight was gone and she felt utterly deflated, like sails no longer pushed full of wind. Dominic was probably in his bed at that very moment, reconciling himself with Fiona, promising her that Sonya meant nothing to him, that it would never happen again, and the two of them would be happy together forever.

The thought made her want to cry fresh tears. Because no matter how much she hated Dominic at that moment, she wanted to be the one in his bed.

No, no, no, and no. You deserve better than him and he doesn't deserve your love, so get over it.

Love? No, she didn't love him. She couldn't love such an arrogant, demanding, thoughtless, cheating jerk. What was there to love? What did he do that was so great she should give him her heart? Nothing she could think of. Let Fiona have him. Let Fiona chase after him and nip at his heels like a little terrier. Let all of her dreams come true. Sonya had her own life, her own dreams, and she lost track of them in the whirlwind that was Dominic. This internship was supposed to be the thing that opened doors and set her on her career path.

Now she knew better. Not only was she done with Dominic, but she was also done with the entire entertainment industry. She didn't want to be an agent or a lawyer. She didn't want to work with men like Dominic or women like Fiona. She didn't want to be objectified and treated like a little slut. *Slut.* The word stung more than the slap across her face.

"Miss? Can I help you?"

The softly spoken question pulled Sonya from her

angry thoughts, and she realized the doorman was staring at her.

"I..."

"Do you need a taxi?"

"Um, yeah, I do. Thank you."

"No problem. Stay in here where it's warm and I'll call one right away."

Sonya self-consciously folded her arms across her chest, but the doorman's eyes were kind and he didn't sound like he was judging her. She supposed he saw worse all the time. Hell, she probably was not the first girl to come down from the fifteenth floor in need of a cab. Why would Dominic treat anybody with a modicum of courtesy and respect?

The doorman appeared again within a few minutes. "There's a car waiting outside."

"Thank you." She automatically checked her purse, realizing that she had absolutely no money with her. She even left her credit card at home because she thought Dominic was taking her out on a date...she thought he would be capable of taking care of her for one night. Well, that was a mistake she was never going to make again. But even the firmest resolution wasn't going to help her now. What was she going to do? Walk all the way to Westwood?

The doorman must have recognized her plight. "Didn't I see you accompany Mr. Barrows last night?"

"Yes."

"I'm sure he intended to see you home safely himself. I'll make sure that everything is taken care of."

Sonya's face burned. Of course, he knew exactly what happened. He would have seen Fiona march right in like she owned the place. "Oh...thank you. You probably have to do this sort of thing often, huh?"

"Ma'am?"

Sonya wished she stopped at *thank you*. "I mean, uh, calling a cab on Mr. Barrows' behalf."

"It is my job to call his car when he's ready to have it brought around. But I've never ordered another young woman a taxi." He leaned forward, the corners of his eyes wrinkling slightly. "Do you know who owns this building?"

"Uh, no."

"Frank Jessup."

"I don't know..."

"Fiona Jessup's father."

"Oh...well...thanks again."

"Just doing my job, ma'am. You have a good day."

Sonya didn't think that was possible. She wasn't sure she'd be having a good day any time in the near future, but the man's sincerely offered words, and a warm smile pulled a small smile from her. She probably wasn't the first broken-hearted girl to show up in his lobby, dressed in rumpled clothes, red-faced and distracted, unprepared for the journey out of the building.

Brokenhearted? Pull yourself together girl.

She walked out of the building with deliberate steps, doing everything she could to leave with a little bit of her dignity intact. She was glad she would never have to come back, that she would never see the doorman again, that this nightmare would soon be over. In a few days, it would feel just like that—like nothing more than a bad dream. And then a few weeks after that, even the feeling of a bad dream would fade away, and perhaps in a few years, she'd be able to look back on the whole ordeal with a certain fondness?

No. That probably would not happen. She shouldn't think of it as anything but a hard lesson learned well. No more men like Dominic. No more bad decisions. No more mistakes like this. She looked down at her hand as she stepped into the too-bright sun, noticing the strands of red entwined through her fingers. She shook her hand, trying to free herself from the reminder of the other woman, but they clung to her. She balled her hand into a fist and shoved it into her pocket, opening the taxi door with the other.

When the driver asked her for the address, she momentarily considered giving the address to her parents' home. She wanted to see her mother, cry on her shoulder and tell her every stupid decision until she was cleansed. Or maybe absolved. But she did not want to see her father. Would it be possible to tell her mother without him finding out that his own boss had been fucking his little girl six ways to Sunday? No. Probably not. She gave her own address and settled against the seat with her eyes closed, praying that the driver wasn't the chatty sort.

Thankfully, he didn't say another word until the taxi stopped in front of her apartment building.

"Uh, the doorman said that he'd make sure it was taken care of," Sonya said as she pushed the door open.

"Yeah, don't worry about it. We talked it over."

"And the tip..."

"Handled."

Sonya pulled herself from the car and slammed the door behind her. The taxi pulled away, leaving her alone and shivering, all the adrenaline from the confrontation with Fiona completely depleted. She wanted a shower. She wanted to sleep. She wanted to cry but she wasn't sure who the tears were for and there was a big block of ice in her throat anyway.

"It'll be fine," she promised herself. "Today is a new day and last night...last night is over."

She kept herself upright, somehow, until she stumbled into her room. Fortunately, her roommate's door was shut against the world, and so she was able to slip in unnoticed. She clawed her clothes off—she'd burn the dress the first chance she got—and fell into her bed with a harsh breath of relief. It almost sounded like a sob, but Sonya was not going to allow herself to cry.

CHAPTER 9

WE ARE NEVER EVER
GETTING BACK TOGETHER

WHEN THE FIRST bouquet of red roses arrived three days after she left Dominic's apartment and two days after she quit her job, Sonya thought it was meant for her roommate. When the second arrived, she thought it had to be a joke. By the time of the third delivery, Sonya was *pissed*. At twelve, she was so livid she was sure steam was coming from her ears. Was this really his way of apologizing? Did he really think that *144 fucking roses* was a way to make up for all the bullshit he put her through? She didn't even like roses—not that he ever bothered to ask her. She wasn't his girlfriend, so why should he care what flowers she liked?

And why was he sending her roses now? The deliveries themselves didn't shed much light on her question. All of the cards were simply addressed to her. A few bore personal messages, but he couldn't even take the time to fill out and sign all twelve of the cards. They created a cloud of cloying perfume in her tiny bedroom and the sight of them filled her with so many negative emotions that she knew she had to get them out of her life. She decided to donate them to the nearby woman's shelter, and no explanation was needed or given. But the woman who helped her carry them into the building gave her a reassuring hug and a thumb's up.

With the summer more than half over, she didn't have any hope of finding another internship. She'd ask her dad for help, but of course, he didn't know the whole story and he was pretty livid that she would walk out on her responsibilities. Her mother reassured her that he would get over it, sooner or later. Sonya wasn't counting on *sooner* and she definitely didn't want to explain what happened. Lying wasn't an option either—he could always tell. So fine, she'd let him simmer and stew away until he was ready to talk to her. She wasn't a little girl anymore, and she had bigger problems than her daddy's opinion of her.

In the first two days after she quit, she made a half-hearted effort to find a paying job, submitting her resume to temp agencies all over town. She hoped they never called her back. Rent wasn't a problem, and she had enough money to live on until school started and her loans came through. She didn't feel like working. She didn't feel like leaving the house. She didn't feel like going out and meeting new people, or talking to the people she already knew. She didn't want to talk about Dominic and she couldn't think about anything else, so that severely limited her conversations.

Sonya caught herself missing him in the odd moments, usually when she wasn't even thinking about him. She'd be focusing on a movie or a book and suddenly it would hit her —she loved the way he kissed her. Or she'd be doing the dishes and she would yearn to feel his hands on the small of her back or gently moving over her breasts. She'd wake up in the middle of the night and be surprised by her solitude, even though she only woke up by his side once.

And then the roses multiplied in her bedroom like tribbles out of control. She imagined a hundred scenarios and in each one, she made it clear exactly where he could stick those flowers and exactly what he could do with them after that. Ultimately, she did nothing. Her only response was silence, and at least they didn't go to waste.

On Thursday, the delivery consisted of candy. Belgium chocolate, to be exact. That was followed by a European tour of toffees, caramels, and other sweet, exotic delights. A few of them were tempting, but she didn't even want to give him the satisfaction of tearing a wrapper open and smelling the perfectly smooth and beautiful mixed chocolate. Not that he would ever know, but it was the principle of the thing. Especially since the candy was just as insulting as the roses. Why couldn't he just write a letter or send her a card? Maybe a fucking text message? Maybe he knew that if he tried to apologize, he would never sound sincere. Did he even know he did anything wrong? That arrogant sono-fabitch probably thought Sonya owed *him* something.

On Friday there was only one knock on the door. Unfortunately, her roommate was home and she answered the door and received the tiny, rectangle box. Unmistakably jewelry, she couldn't even wait to close the door before ripping it open.

"Sonya, you won't believe this...Also, I'm sorry for opening your package, but I was dying of curiosity."

"I don't care. You can have it."

"Um, I don't think you mean that."

"I'm pretty sure that's exactly what I mean. I wouldn't have said it if I didn't mean it."

"I'm not going to hold you to that because you haven't *seen* it."

"I don't even care what it is. Keep it. Sell it. Throw it in the garbage. I don't care."

"Oh, nobody's going to be throwing this away." She lifted the diamond tennis bracelet from the box, letting it drape over her fingers, the tiny, perfect jewels glittering in the light. "This must have cost him a fortune."

"Oh, you're right. Here, let me see."

She handed it over without protest, and Sonya slid it into her pocket without a second glance. "They'll love this at the shelter."

"You're not really going to donate that, are you?"

"Yes, I really am."

"Why?"

"I don't want it."

"Let me have it back."

"No. You had your chance. Besides, are you really going to take that money away from a woman's shelter? What kind of monster are you?"

"The kind of monster that lives in the dark, apparently. What the hell is going on here, Sonya?"

"Nothing. It's none of your business."

"So it is something, you're just laboring under the mistaken notion that your business isn't my business. Is it from your boss?"

"Ex-boss."

"What did he do? I kind of thought you two were going pretty hot and heavy."

"He's a world-class asshole and I'm better off without him."

"What did he do?"

Sonya sighed and returned to the couch. She had her laptop open to a handful of browser windows, each one with a different instruction video. She had all kinds of time on her hands these days and she wanted to learn how to knit. She could make scarves and hats for the shelter, and the homeless shelter, too. First, though, she had to figure out how to get the yarn onto the needles. She also needed to buy needles. Maybe she'd pawn the bracelet, buy her knitting supplies, and donate the rest.

"A sigh isn't an answer. Now I haven't been pushing for information all week, but come on, the dude sent you a diamond bracelet."

"Let's see. First, he basically acted like he was entitled to fuck me any time he liked, but I don't really blame him for that because it's not like I ever told him no. Second, he gave me away like I'm just some whore...and he didn't even care how I felt about it. The only reason nothing happened was that *he* got jealous. And then he takes us back to his place so his fiancé could catch us in bed and slap me in the face for being a slut. Is that enough for you? Do I have your approval now?"

She held her hands up. "Whoa, hey, you know I'm on your side. He sounds like a real asshole, and yeah, you shouldn't keep the bracelet. I'm sorry that you had to go through that. You weren't...you weren't *hurt*, were you?"

"No. No, I didn't get hurt." Not like she meant, anyway. "And now he's sending me all this stuff like I'm so stupid and shallow he can get in my pants again if he just spends enough money. I don't even know why he's bothering me now. He has Fiona."

"Maybe he doesn't."

"What?"

"Maybe he dumped her. Maybe he's single now and he wants you."

"She's pregnant."

"Is the baby his?"

"Uh, yeah, pretty sure it's his. It doesn't matter. I deserve to be treated better than that."

"Do you want to go out tonight?"

Her face is twisted. "Ugh. No. I'm definitely not in the mood to see or talk to or meet anybody."

"Who said anything about meeting anybody? You just quit your job lady, you need to go out and get drunk. That's all. Just good old-fashioned drinking, nothing too crazy. And definitely no men."

"I'll think about it."

"No, there's nothing to think about. We're going out tonight and that's final."

Sonya nodded. "Fine." She didn't have the energy to fight about it. "I'll need a stiff drink anyway."

"Why?"

"Because I've got to tell Dominic to stop sending me all this bullshit."

"Are you going to call him or go down to his office?"

Sonya blanched. She didn't like the idea of either one, honestly. Though it was far less dangerous to call. If she went to his office, everybody would see her, including her father, and if things got heated, everybody would hear them, too. So. Calling.

She knew how to get through his direct line, bypassing his receptionist. He answered on the third ring.

"Stop sending me flowers. No more candy. No more *jewelry*. I'm serious, Dominic. I don't want to hear from you again."

"Sonya, wait..."

"*No*. Fuck. Didn't you hear me the first time? In case you didn't, allow me to repeat myself. Fuck. You. I hope you and your bitch fiancee are very happy together. Really, I do. Now fuck off."

"Sonya--"

She hung up, cutting him off. Almost immediately, the

phone came alive in her hand. She swiped the screen, declining the call and sending it straight to voice mail. Whatever he had to tell her, it didn't matter. She didn't think anything he had to say would matter. She wasn't interested in any of it. And she congratulated herself for being so clear on it, confident that he would leave her in peace now.

What she didn't remember was that Dominic was like a shark. When there was something he wanted, he went after it until it was his. A trait that made him a great success in business and in his personal life, and now the full force of his attention was turned onto her. Ignoring the problem wouldn't make it go away. A fact she learned when the knock on her door wasn't announcing a new delivery but Dominic himself.

Sonya squared her shoulders and folded her arms over her chest. Dominic looked...different. He was always perfection personified, everything from his hair to his shoes completely immaculate. Even when they were fooling around in his office or the back of his car, he never actually looked rumpled or even remotely out of sorts. Sonya had never been privy to his morning regimen, but she imagined that it must have taken him hours in the morning to put him together.

He looked like shit.

Well, for Dominic. His hair wasn't gelled. His jacket wasn't buttoned. His shirt wasn't ironed. His shoes were scuffed. He had stubble on his jaw and upper lip.

"What do you want?"

"I want to talk."

"I've already said everything I've had to say to you."

"I still have more things to say to you."

"I don't care. I'm done listening. I've listened to you too much. And what did it get me?"

"I know, and I understand why you're angry. You have every right to be angry with me."

"Goddamned right I do. And do you really think that some flowers and a bracelet will change anything? I don't know what kind of girl you're used to dealing with...actually, I do. How's your fiancee?" Sonya asked with a sugar-sweet smile.

"She's not my fiancee anymore."

"She's still the mother of your child."

"No, she's not that either. We agreed it would be best if we parted ways."

"Whose baby is it then? How do you know it's not yours?"

"She's not pregnant. A bit crazy, but not pregnant."

"Well, congratulations I guess. And now you're bugging me because you're so lonely? Find another idiot to buy what you're selling." She moved to slam the door but he was too quick, catching the door before she could slam it in his face.

"If you would just let me explain..."

"What do you think you could possibly say to me? What do you think will make a difference to me? You gave me to some dirtbag and then you let your fiancee slap me in the face. You've treated me like shit...like your whore...and I *loved* you." She slapped her palm over her mouth, her eyes widening as she realized what she said. Loved? No, no, she didn't love him. She was in lust with him. She was in love with being in love. She loved the attention. She loved the ego boost. She did *not* love him.

But she made the mistake of saying the words and she could tell from the look on Dominic's face that he was about to pounce on that mistake.

"I know what I did was shitty. I know I treated you terribly...and I don't expect you to forgive me right away. But I'm not going to just leave you alone, either."

She snorted. "Of course, you're not. Get out of here. Get out of here and leave me alone, okay? We didn't have anything except..."

"How can you say that?" Dominic cut in.

"Just...just go away. Just go away and leave me alone. We're done. Really, completely finished." She yanked the door from his grip and then slammed it shut, leaving him standing alone in the hallway, her heart hammering in her ears. She quickly locked the door and leaned heavily against the solid wood, gasping for breath as she tried to get herself under control again.

"This is for the best. This is for the best. This is for the best." She repeated the words until the urge to cry passed. But it didn't pass. Not really. It just settled like a heavy stone in her throat. Why did everything have to be such a mess?

He knocked.

She ignored him.

He knocked again.

She ignored him.

He pounded on the door like a cop, hard enough to shake the frame, and long enough to make her realize that he was not just going to go away.

Sonya yanked the door open again. "Will you stop it? Somebody is going to call the police. I have neighbors."

"If you let me in, we won't be disturbing them anymore."

"If they call the cops, you're the one who's going to get hauled away."

"I won't be hauled anywhere. This is ridiculous, Sonya. Please, just give me ten minutes."

"What difference do you think ten minutes will make?"

"If you don't think it'll make any difference, why won't you let me in? If you hate me so much I can never say anything to win you over, then ten minutes seems like a pretty small price to pay for a lifetime of peace."

"So if I listen to you for ten minutes, you'll leave me alone for the rest of my life?"

"Yes."

"No more flowers?"

"No more flowers."

"No more chocolate, or bracelets, or bullshit?"

"Cross my heart and hope to die."

"Fine, get in here. Talk fast. The clock is ticking." She took her phone from her pocket and set the timer on the clock before holding it up so he could see the numbers tick down.

"I know there's nothing you really want to hear from me right now. And I know the flowers and the bracelet...none of that's going to change anything."

"Then why did you waste your money and my time?"

"Because I wanted you to know that I'm thinking about you. I think about you all the time, Sonya. And I mean that. All of the time. Every day. Since the first moment, I saw you, which was not at the club, by the way. I miss you at work. I miss you when I go home."

"I'm sorry to hear that but I'm sure you can find somebody else to torment and humiliate. Maybe even somebody who is better at sucking dick than I am."

"I don't want to torment and humiliate you. And I don't believe that I'm ever going to find anybody who is better at what you do. Sonya, I know I fucked up in so many ways. But I want to prove to you how sorry I am. How much I miss you. How much I need you."

She shook her head. "You can't."

"Give me a chance to try."

"What do you think you're going to do?"

He put his hand in his jacket pocket and produced a pair of handcuffs.

"If you think I'm going to let you use those things on me, you're crazy."

"They're not for you."

"What?"

He pulled the strap of his messenger bag off his shoulder and handed it over to her. "I've used everything in this bag on you at least once. Sometimes to punish you. Now I want you to use them on me. To punish me."

"You want me to punish you?"

"No, but I deserve to be punished. And you deserve to be the one that dishes it out."

"I don't want..."

"Yes, you do. You want to make me hurt like all those times I made you hurt. You want to see me bruised and bleeding and begging. This is your chance, Sonya. A chance nobody else has ever had and not one I'm going to offer a second time." He held the bag out to her. "I suggest you don't waste the opportunity."

"I don't see how this is going to change anything."

"Maybe it'll make us both feel better. You never know unless you try."

She reached out for it, not sure what she intended to do, not even when she was lifting the strap over her shoulder. His eyes were steady, and she tried to return his gaze just as calmly, but her heart was racing, and her palms were sweaty and tingly. They stared at each other for several beats before Sonya realized he was waiting for instructions from her. He wasn't going to move until she heard her give the command.

"Take off your coat."

He immediately shrugged it away and draped it over the back of the couch. He seemed much taller in her little apartment, his shoulders broader and his thighs thicker.

"Get completely naked."

He obediently stripped, pulling the clothes from his limbs and over his head until he stood before her in all his glory. She caught her breath; her eyes drinking in the sight of him, even though she wanted to play it cool and act like she didn't care. Like she was completely indifferent. She was far from indifferent to his beauty, and longing flared inside of her. This was all part of his master plan to trick her, she was sure of it. He'd make his move once her brain was appropriately jellified, dazzled by his sharply defined body, his dusting of black hair over thick, deep pecs.

I wasn't going to do this again. I wasn't going to be in this situation again.

But it wasn't the same situation. Not quite. Not really. Because for once, she held all the cards. And for once, she was going to show him how it feels to be broken.

CHAPTER 10

BEAUTY AND A BEAT

SONYA GESTURED for Dominic to follow her, leading him into her bedroom and closing the door behind them.

"Kneel," Sonya commanded, doing her best to keep her voice even.

She was shaking from head to toe, could feel the quivering deep in her ribs, with every trembling breath. She felt more than nervous. More than excited. His eyes locked with hers as he began to sink to the floor and the weight pulled at her chest. She felt like she was standing naked in front of him. Felt like he could see right through to the center of her.

"Put your hands behind your back. Don't look at me."

Dominic's shoulders flexed as he held his hands together behind his back, his head down and eyes averted. At first, she couldn't pull her gaze away from him. His body was perfect, and her attention slid lower to his cock, which was already half-erect against his thigh. For some reason, she never expected him to actually enjoy it. The answering tingle between her legs alerted her to the fact that he definitely wasn't the only one.

She took a deep breath and forced her attention to the

rather large duffel bag he handed her. She unzipped it, pulling the sides open to reveal tightly coiled ropes, gleaming black leather whips, the glint of handcuffs, ball gags, a round object that looked like it came from the dentist's office used to pry open a jaw, a pink feather duster —the sight of which surprised a laugh out of her—and a blindfold.

"Do you want me to use all these things on you?"

"I want you to do what you need to do."

She paced in a circle around him. What she needed to do? Sonya had no idea what it would take. Did he deserve to be beaten for what he did? Was physical violence really necessary?

"Can I say something?" Dominic asked.

Sonya nodded and then realized he couldn't see her. "Yes."

"There aren't many people who could say they had me on their knees. I'm turning myself over to you, Sonya. I'm asking you to let me serve your will. I'm not telling you what to do. Tell me what you want, even if you really want me to leave."

"I don't want you to leave." She licked her dry lips. "Stay where you are. Don't move."

Sonya dropped the bag on the bed and backed her way into the bathroom, kicking the door shut behind her. She moved slowly, deliberately, taking her time and not hurrying a single breath. She picked up the comb first and dragged the teeth through her hair, working the tangles free and catching the flyaways for the first time in days. She quickly twisted it into a tight braid and secured it with a rubber band, letting it fall between her shoulder blades.

She tugged her shirt over her head and unclasped her bra. She opened the closet door and retrieved her special black bra and lacy panties, pulling the articles of clothes on quickly and studying her reflection. Black eyeliner and red lipstick were the final touches, and she squared her shoulders. The more she looked at the part, the more she felt the part, and when she emerged from the bathroom, she had a new swagger in her walk. Dominic was exactly as she left him.

"Come here, boy."

He crawled to her, stopping once he reached her feet. She lifted her foot, wiggling her toes in front of his face. "You're nothing. Not even fit to lick the ground I stand on. Are you good enough to lick my toes?" She pushed her foot into his mouth. "Show me." She felt a twinge of anxiety as she forced her toes past his lips. Was this good?

The second his velvety tongue slid between her toes, the twinge she felt brightened into a pang of pleasure. It wasn't that her toes were so sensitive—though the wet caress did feel better than she expected—it was the immediate response to her request. As he said, he only wanted to serve her. She recognized that desire. Knew she harbored it as well, had bent to Dominic's will so many times precisely because of the deeply held desire she had to submit to him. She closed her fist in his hair, gripping it tightly to keep herself upright, pressing his mouth down to the bend of her toes.

His hot mouth slipped over each digit and then along the arch of her foot. He bit at her gently before kissing over the marks again, using his tongue and lips to lather her with attention. Her arm flexed, her fingers tightening around the silky strands, a sharp, unnameable sensation shooting up from the bottom of her foot to the juncture between her thighs.

He cupped her heel and lowered her foot to the floor

then picked up the other. His tongue was slippery and warm between her toes, awakening new sensations and sending chills down her spine. "Do you like this, boy?"

"Yes--"

"Louder."

"*Yes*, Mistress."

"Stand up."

He released her foot and obediently rose, towering over her. She wrapped her arms around his neck. "Take me to bed."

He swooped her up from the floor, easily cradling her in his arms. He brought her to the bed, depositing her on the mattress with far more tenderness than she ever would have expected. She caught her panties and wiggled them off her hips. His fingers curled around the flimsy material and he dragged them down her legs and over her feet. She fisted his hair and pulled him between her thighs, guiding his head to her wet pussy. His tongue flicked over the wet folds, lightly at first. Not what she wanted. She tightened her grip and pressed his mouth against her.

His hands rested on her thighs as he laved his tongue over her clit, coaxing more and more blood to her center until she was throbbing against the hot, velvet of his mouth. He sucked her clit between his lips and she twisted his hair, easing him back. He immediately followed her unspoken order, releasing the nub and returning to long, sweet licks over her tender skin, finding new ways to ignite her nerves.

For a long time, she wanted nothing more than that slow exploration. She controlled each gesture, each flick of his tongue, guiding them on a winding, garden path to her orgasm. He was responsive to each cue, and it was like using a vibrator, but better because it was his tongue and his breath warming her skin and his soft moans making her flesh vibrate. Every other time, he'd done exactly what he wanted to do, touched her how he wanted, told her how she wanted to feel, and he was so good at it that she always believed him. Now she realized she could believe him when he said he was turning himself over to her.

But how long would this submission last? She didn't want to be chained to his will, jerked around by him without warning, and then placated again with some sort of demonstration of affection or submission. She didn't want this to become a pattern for the two of them...but she couldn't deny that at that very moment, his submission felt better than good....it felt *right*.

She brought herself right to the brink of orgasm and yanked his head back, staring down at glazed eyes and glossy lips.

"Are you hard," she asked huskily.

"Yes, Mistress."

She finally released her grip, her fingers aching a little with the sudden release of tension. "Show me."

He pushed himself up to his knees, leaning back slightly so she could see the way his dick jutted in front of him, the head as slick and glossy as his mouth. Pre-come slid down his shaft in tiny, clear drops, his skin already flushes a deep pink. She sat up, leaning over to cup his balls, rolling her fingers around them gently. She squeezed slightly, watching his face to gauge his reaction, and then increased the pressure. He sucked his breath in, and his eyes widened slightly, but both reactions were subtle. Curious, Sonya clenched hard enough to make his jaw tighten, but he didn't make a sound, didn't try to escape the pain. His duffel bag of tricks started to make more sense.

She released him and gestured at the bed. "Lay down on your back."

Sonya, who didn't know the first thing about tying safe knots, wasn't sure she could secure him with the rope, but there were cuffs in the bag. She locked him down to the bed, cuffing his ankles to the footboard and his wrists directly over his head. He watched every moment from beneath heavy eyes, his magnificent body laid out before her, entirely hers for the taking. She was pretty sure nobody had ever seen him so vulnerable. But it was more than his vulnerability that made her pulse jump. He wasn't vulnerable to anybody else in the world—only to her.

She returned to the bag and doubt crept back. She'd never used any of this stuff before. What if she hurt him?

Isn't that the point? A voice that sounded suspiciously like Dominic's asked from the back of her mind.

Hurt, yes, she countered, *but no damage.*

It's not like I ever held myself back with you. Did I seem terribly worried about inflicting permanent damage?

No, he hadn't seemed very worried. And Sonya didn't know how permanent it was, but he had inflicted some damage. The betrayal she felt, the anger and humiliation, wasn't gone, and Dominic had meant for her to exorcise that. All of it. To drain it from her system before it went septic and ruined her chance at happiness.

Despite the justification, she did pick a flogger made out of soft suede. He'd used that very same flogger on her before, and she felt comfortable wielding it. She could have secured his face down, but she was too fascinated by the look in his eyes as she stood over him. Sonya wanted to see him where every second of it. His cock was still rock solid, twitching as his tight muscles spasmed with anticipation. She itched to touch him, itched to glide her fingers over the taut skin and tease him or take the pain away. But she wanted him to wait, wanted to drive him into agony before finally offering the release of a caress or a kiss.

She walked from one side of the bed to the other, considering her angles, considering the way his skin stretched across his body in an unbroken, beautiful plain. She focused on his right pec, raising the flogger and bringing it down with a heavy *thud*. Sonya hadn't been trying to hurt him; she was just testing the force. He didn't visibly react, but a rosy blush spread over his chest. She zeroed in on the same spot, bringing the flogger down with more force. The sound of leather hitting skin sent a sharp pang through her, giving her a sense of pleasure she never tasted before.

"You like it, don't you?" His words slithered from beneath the crack of the third blow.

"Yes."

"You didn't know?"

She shook her head. She hadn't known. Not at all. Not even a little bit. How could she have ever expected it?

Sonya hit him again. "How does it feel?" She was a quick learner, and the familiar *thawp* followed one after the other in a quicker and quicker rhythm. "Does it hurt?"

"Each one feels like a kiss, sweetheart."

She bounced the long, suede tails to the other side of his chest, then back to the original blow point, her confidence increasing with each soft *thud*. Soon both pecs were the same shade of deep red, matching blooming roses. She dropped the flogger and skimmed her fingers overheated flesh. He took a deep breath, his spine arching ever so slightly from the mattress. Smiling slightly, she bent to skim her lips along the same path her fingers took, tasting the heat and salt of his sweat.

Sonya tossed the flogger to the foot of the bed and returned to the duffel bag, digging through until she found a stiff black, leather cane, a dozen straps twining together from the base to the tip. She slapped it experimentally against her palm, and even though she barely used any force, it left quite a sting. Sonya blinked in surprise and smiled, wondering how it would sting on tenderized skin. Wondering if it would feel more like a bite than a kiss.

She took a small detour on the way to the bed, turning on her iPod's *Dance Dance Dance* playlist. The bass erupted, vibrating through the walls, masking the sound of her own racing heart. She tapped his chest with the leather, not hard enough to draw a sound. She bounced the cane up and down his torso, subtly increasing the pressure while the blows came faster and faster. He gritted his teeth, twisted and arched, and closed his eyes like he couldn't stand to look at her for another moment. She followed the rhythm of the song, not breaking the chain, feeling the tension in each flick of her wrist.

Red ribbons tore across his chest, crossing back and forth, each new one glowing red and brighter and hotter than the one before. He seemed impervious, as though the welts were no more than skin deep and he didn't even feel the pain along his nerve endings. But all that changed when she targeted his nipple with the hardpoint. She couldn't quite suppress her smile when she hit the delicate skin, his abrupt groan going straight to her clit, making her throb all the more.

"God," she murmured.

"Do it again, Mistress, please."

She dragged the tip over his peaked nipple. "Do you want more?"

"Yes, please, Mistress. Please."

A large part of her was pleased to have pleased him and desperately wanted to do it again. Her desire to satisfy him would always be a large part of their relationship, even if she was at loss to explain exactly why. But today wasn't about *his* desire, according to his own stipulations, and she circled his nipple again, letting the leather linger over every tiny ridge of skin.

"No."

His protesting moan was slight, but she still heard it. "Excuse me. What was that? Are you complaining about my decision?"

"No, Mistress, no."

"Are you sure? Because it sure *sounded* like you had a complaint. Are you disappointed?"

"Please, Mistress, it felt so good. I only wanted more because everything you do feels so good."

"Oh, aren't you sweet? If that's the case, then this should feel like heaven." She was standing over his groin, and he saw her intent but he was completely helpless, unable to block her or push her away or do anything to act in defense of his cock. Even though he knew what she intended to do, his cock was still hard and dripping and almost angry looking.

Dominic screamed when she brought the cane down, his body jerking in response to the hardest blow yet. The welt was immediate, and for the first time, she felt a twinge of regret. She dropped the cane without a second thought, forgetting that she meant to prolong his suffering, forgetting that a second earlier, all she wanted to do was hurt him. She forgot everything except soothing him, taking the pain away. She licked the welt and blew a gentle stream of air over the damp skin, cooling it. He whimpered as her mouth traveled over the red welt, and she followed it across his shaft, and then licked a gentle line from the base to the tip. Pre-come was gathering at his head, the salty flavor startling her into licking him again. She used the tip of her tongue to clean the fluid from his crown, licking until the taste of salt faded, then gripping the head and gently coaxing more liquid from the tip.

The quality of his moans changed. The rumble came from deep within his chest, each sound building and building until it surrounded her, wrapped tightly around her like his strong arms. She lifted her head to see him staring down at her with heavy, dark eyes. Her pussy clenched at the heat in their depths, every inch of her body yearning for his. Her fingers closed around his dick, and she felt his pulse through the thick, velvet-soft flesh, her own heartbeat matching the rapid tempo. Would straddling him and taking him by satisfying her desires? Or his? She was supposed to be punishing him, but riding him like a pony into the sunset wasn't a punishment...

At least, she hoped he didn't view that as a punishment.

"Sonya..." His voice was a rasp of sound, rough as sandpaper dragging down her spine. She licked her lips and tasted him again, sending another sharp spike of lust through her. Her clit throbbed and she had to shift her weight, pressing her thighs together and squirming against the sudden pressure between her legs.

"What you want...and what I want...is the same. It's always been the same. That's why we're so good together." Sonya heard a note of pleading in his voice that she'd never noted before. Splayed and bound before her, covered in welts that would form into bruises, vulnerable to every moment of pain she could choose to inflict. Stripped down to his essence.

And that was all he had to say.

Sonya caught her breath, understanding enfolding her. She bent her head again, closed her eyes, and opened her lips, allowing her mouth to make a connection with his flesh again. She didn't think she didn't plot her actions or analyze her own motives, she just moved. To the rhythm of the music, to the rhythm of his pulse. Moved like a stream of water cutting its own path to the river. Moved her mouth up and down his cock, the shaft heaving on her tongue, then moved up his body, following the heat of each bruise like a roadmap.

A road map that ultimately led to his glistening lips.

He latched onto her mouth as soon as she was within touching distance, burying his tongue between her lips, drinking deeply of her, like a man dying for any drop of moisture, every second of sustenance. She buried her hands in his hair, pressing her fingernails against his scalp and giving as good as she got, the temperature beneath her skin rising. She felt like she was melting, her thighs slick and buttery, sweat rolling down her neck, getting caught in her hair. He was slick, too, and she positioned herself over him, grinding her aching flesh down on his cock. Her clit glided against the ridge, the pleasure from that pressure instant and addicting. Her hips swiveled, picking up speed, and she began to rock, the friction igniting her senses and burning through her blood.

"Fuck me, baby, please fuck me. Please, baby."

"Do you need me?"

"I need you baby. Please. Fuck me."

Sonya caught his chin in a firm grip and looked into his eyes, locking their gazes and holding his attention. His eyes remained on hers. He didn't even blink.

"Nobody else. Nobody else, Dominic, ever again."

"Nobody else," he promised. "Only you."

"Don't make empty promises, Dominic." Emotion made her voice heavy. She could hear the strain under her own words, and she tried to swallow, but her throat was tight. So tight it almost hurt to swallow, and she knew the emotion was heavy in her eyes, too.

"Only you. Sonya, sweetheart, only you."

"You want me to fuck you?"

"*Please.*"

She reached behind her, gripping his thick cock and guiding the head to her swollen, tender flesh. He slid into her easily, her body welcoming him deep inside. She rocked back until she was fully seated, her breath catching in her throat every time his solid flesh jerked against her walls.

"Do it...oh Sonya, baby, do it."

She sat up straight, her hands resting on his flat stomach, her hair falling down her back, feeling like a thousand tiny fingers stroking over her skin. He didn't move. He didn't rise up to meet her. He didn't try to coax her into rocking. His fingers were curled into tight fists, and she wanted to unlock the cuffs so he could hold her, so he could grip her arms with bruising strength, sink his fingertips into her flesh until he left black and blue crescents.

She slid her palms up to his chest, bracing herself against his solid pecs and rising up, losing his amazing length inch by slow, agonizing inch. She missed him immediately, felt empty and frustrated, her entire body *clenching*, demanding his return. When she felt nothing but the tip at her slick entrance, she slammed herself down. He groaned. She gasped, fireworks erupting in her mind, in her lower stomach, in her thighs, the sparks erupting everywhere.

Sonya used her entire body, her muscles flexing, holding him down, holding him in place, holding him inside of her. Could she hold him like that forever? He felt more like a wild animal like she was trying to tame a force of nature. It seemed as silly as extracting a promise from a lion that he wouldn't feed or trying to lasso a tornado and keep it in the backyard. But she wanted to try.

God, she really wanted to try.

Her mouth found his again, tongue plunging deep past his lips as she sank down on his cock. Her hands moved to his shoulders and energy charged through her hips, bringing her to new heights. Bringing them both to new epiphanies. He absorbed that energy and reflected it back, taking over when she started to wane, bucking beneath her like a stallion. She tightened her knees into his side, digging into his hips with each powerful, breathtaking thrust.

Sonya had been treated to a thousand types of pleasure at Dominic's hands. He'd been gentle and rough, slow and fast, demanding and giving. He'd sparked orgasms with nothing more than a kiss on the back of her neck. He'd pounded into her until something snapped inside and the resulting orgasm was a flood erupting from a broken dam. She'd felt it quickly and she felt it building slowly. She'd been shocked and cajoled and even with reams and reams of field research, of memories and analysis, of physical, body memory, she still didn't know what to expect. She still didn't know what was happening to her, still couldn't anticipate the light pulsing, growing in the very center of her.

The more he tried to take control with his body, the more she resisted, the more she demanded from him. They were two halves coming together as one, but that union could have been a dance or a fight, reconciliation or a war. Sonya couldn't tell the difference, couldn't see where the lines were drawn. Couldn't even see the lines separating their physical selves. He was inside of her, but she felt like she was sinking into him, melding their bodies together. When he surged, she surged, when he bucked and slammed up, she matched him precisely, moving in the opposite direction.

And somehow, the more she fought him, the better it was. They harmonized. Like the music drowning out their moans, driving them with the intoxicating, hypnotizing beat. She could look him in the eyes. She could bite and kiss and scratch. She could demand more, take it all, and then slam her body down with enough force to make him gasp. His body could take it, the muscles rippling beneath his smooth skin *begging* for all that and so much more.

When Sonya finally reached the breaking point, she shouted. But it was unlike any shout she'd ever heard from her own throat, unlike any sound she'd ever made. It was more of a growl, a bear emerging from her dark, winter cave with her cubs in tow, or a lioness taking down a zebra for the entire pride. It was raw with unshed tears and rough with pleasure that was fully, completely unleashed for the first time. It was deep, primitive, and not without fear. Not without tears. It took her by surprise, echoing in her ears and reverberating in her chest long after the sound stopped and the tidal wave of pleasure eased back, retracting until she was empty and shivering, washed clean of so much of the pain that had infected her since she allowed Dominic to take her heart.

CHAPTER 11

GIVE IT ALL WE GOT TONIGHT

WHEN DOMINIC WOKE UP, his wrists were once again bound to the headboard, and Sonya was sitting on the edge of the mattress, her hair pulled back from her face, her eyes heavy from lack of sleep. He smiled up at her, an uneasy heaviness settling in his stomach when she didn't return the gesture. She looked more beautiful than ever, her neck covered in purple marks, her lips swollen from a night of passionate kisses. He unconsciously licked the corner of his mouth, imagining the pressure and soft taste of her lips. He had the feeling that there wouldn't be any kissing for a while.

"I want to know all of it." She arched her brow at him, challenging him to deny her. "Every detail. Your whole life."

"Right now?" His stomach growled and his bladder felt a little heavy. He didn't think he could concentrate on a tale of that magnitude, but Sonya didn't look like she was going to budge on this point. She wanted to know everything, and he didn't blame her, but still. "That's a lot of talking before breakfast."

"The highlights, at least." Her eyes narrowed slightly as she searched his face. He didn't think she realized it, but she always looked at him with such naked curiosity. Her feelings were always mirrored in her eyes, an open book for him to read. Despite their night together, there was still fear in the blue depths, still confused. "I don't know who you really are, Dominic. I know that you and I...we have a connection. I know I *feel* something with you and I don't feel it with anybody else. I know you feel something for me, or you wouldn't be here right now. But...I don't even know if I like you. I'm sorry, that sounds...bitchy but...."

"No, don't be sorry." She never sounded bitchy to him. Maybe it was because the anger came from a legitimate place. If he could go back in time and do everything differently with her, he would in a heartbeat. He'd change it all, from their first meeting up to that very second. For one thing, he wouldn't have attempted to exorcise his anger and frustration on her. He owed her an explanation. He owed her more than that. Especially since he didn't want to lose the one chance he might have at happiness. "Come here. Might as well get comfortable. This is going to be a long story."

She settled in at his side, relaxing against him on her next breath. Her hair tickled his chin and nose a little bit, but he inhaled deeply anyway, catching the smell of her strawberry shampoo beneath the combination of sleep and sweat and sex. He ached to put his arm around her and hold her closer. He wished she hadn't resecured the cuffs. It felt like it would be so much easier to talk to her if he could hold her, anchor himself to her.

"When I was fourteen, my parents passed away."

The story didn't have a happy beginning, but very few of Dominic's stories *did*. He'd only been so professionally successful because his personal life was often in a state of shambles, and the rot began that long-ago winter day, when his parents' car spun out on black ice, sending them into oncoming traffic. He'd been at school, and it was Miriam, his godmother, who came to pick him up that day with streaked makeup and a deep frown pulling her mouth tight.

"My godparents took me in, and they took very good care of me." He never wanted for anything after that. They let him claim any room he wanted in their ten-thousand square foot mansion in the Hollywood Hills. They showered him with gifts, clothes, cars, and expensive trips. Anything he asked for, they were happy to provide. Frank Jessup even promised to give him a job and maybe even make him a partner at his agency, where he handled contract and entertainment law. "But I never felt like a member of the family. My parents were gone and I didn't have anybody else. Still, I can't fault the Jessups. They tried." Sonya lifted her head, and Dominic nodded. "That's right. I've known Fiona for a very long time."

Dominic watched her face as she processed that news— the slight quirk of her eyebrow and the new tightness around her lips. "Have you been with her since you were fourteen?"

"No. And yes. In a way. She's two years older than me and we always had...a connection."

The first time he saw his new "foster sister," she was sunbathing beside the pool in the skimpiest white bikini Dominic had ever seen, before or since. Her body had been perfect, her hair a shade of cherry-gold he'd never seen before, and he was a walking, seething cauldron of hormones. Even with his heart broken and his mind shattered by grief, his body knew what it wanted, knew what mattered. The connection they shared was the most basic one of all—pure lust—and it wasn't long before the feeling was mutual.

"It wasn't easy to live in that house." Even though it was a massive house and he had plenty of room. "She...well, she was something. I avoided her. I had to. Every time I saw her, I had very inappropriate thoughts." Thoughts that she probably suspected from the beginning. He wasn't exactly suave and subtle about it—what teenage boy was when it came to his first full-fledged crush? Especially when that crush was fueled by hormones and grief. "I kept telling myself it was nothing I would ever act on, that she was practically family, but it got harder and harder. She finally left for Berkeley and I thought I was in the clear...until she came back on her winter break."

"So you were what? Sixteen?"

"I just turned seventeen." And was still a virgin, much to his shame. He wanted to have some first-hand knowledge of what to do before he kissed her. But she took the choice out of his hands by kissing him, guiding his hand to her breast, and cupping the growing bulge beneath his pants.

"I was never with anybody else before her. None of the other girls were...they weren't her. I'd rather sit at home alone in my room, thinking about how I shouldn't be thinking about her walking out of the bathroom in her bra and panties than go out with girls who actually liked me."

"Did you make the first move or did she?"

"She did. I never would have. She kissed me and then we--"

"Okay, I don't need to hear the sordid details."

"Fair enough."

It wasn't exactly a memory he wanted to relive. Their first kiss had been awkward, to say the very least. His teeth got in the way. He squeezed her tit a little too hard. He fell all over himself trying to get his clothes off, and he tore her blouse in the process. At the time, he'd been too caught up in the moment to realize how terrible everything was, but hindsight was twenty/twenty, and with that benefit, he could see he was nothing more than an overeager, clumsy puppy.

"After that, everything was different. She went back to school, but I was completely in love. It was real...disgusting. I promised her I'd wait for her, and I did."

"What about her? Did she wait for you while she was gone?"

"Oh, I doubt it. I never asked. It never occurred to me that she *would* and I didn't care. As long as she was with me when she came home. The two of us just...we had a lot of energy. A lot of time and energy. She never wanted anything more, never seemed interested in the two of us being together. And I...I kept waiting for her. For years. All through college and law school."

"You were in love with her the whole time," Sonya said softly, more of a statement than a question. Love. It was strange how little he used that word. Even when his entire world revolved around her, he never used it--never said it, never thought it. Maybe because he wasn't exactly senti-mental. Maybe because it never exactly felt like love. Lust and yearning and desire and anger and passion, yes. But they hardly ever spoke to each other, hardly ever spent time together with their clothes on.

"Yeah, I guess so. That seems like one way to explain it. When I moved to New York for law school, she told me she thought we should see other people." A suggestion he happily agreed to, even though the thought of her with any other man made his blood simmer and boil. "I tried to date, but I didn't have the time or the energy. Nobody else caught my attention, and I was so busy with school. That's when I started looking into the scene."

"The scene?"

"BDSM clubs. Of which there are many in New York. It was the perfect escape. I didn't want to let anybody close. Didn't want to let anybody mess with my head the way she did, mostly because I wasn't done letting her. But I could go to a club or a party and dominate anybody I wanted and then never talk to them again."

Every girl had been wearing Fiona's face. Everyone he whipped and lashed, spanked and paddled, tortured and teased. Every girl had absorbed the punishment meant for her, and the happy little masochists had loved him for it. His reputation preceded him, and before long, they all sought him out, eager to submit.

"That sounds rather...empty."

Emotionally, it had been. Physically, however, it had been spectacular. It was a wonderful way to relieve stress and decompress after all the pressure of school, and it didn't take long to convince himself that it was *all* he needed. He didn't need Fiona, he didn't need a steady relationship in his life, and he didn't need to be with somebody who knew him, who cared for him. The loneliness inside of him since his parents' accident only grew, sinking deeper and deeper into his soul.

"It was," he admitted. He would have never said as much to anybody else, but she already knew the truth. "I told myself it was for the best. The people were great, and the lifestyle is fulfilling in its own way, but I wanted...I wanted her. That it was all I really wanted. I did make a few friends...and there was one girl who could have been some-thing special, but I was still too hung up over Fiona to do anything about it. I called her as soon as I came back to LA, but she didn't answer. And I fucking *waited* for her call."

For days. Friends from school wanted to go out and see him, but he turned down invitations and ignored blatant come-ons because he wanted to be ready when she called. Because except for one night at the end of his first year in New York, he hadn't seen her the entire time he was in school. Because he still dreamed about her at night, still saw her face on all of his slaves and pets, and still needed to talk to somebody who actually *knew* him.

It was sad that Fiona was the only person who fit all those criteria but hardly surprising. Not when she was the only person he could see for so many years.

"When she finally did call me, she was all apologies. She told me she needed to see me and we decided to take a long weekend in San Diego. She likes the beaches there." Of course, he and Fiona had fucked that weekend, trying to squeeze in three years' worth of lust in forty-eight hours. But there was more than sex, and even now, Dominic would consider that one of the happiest weekends of his life. In those forty-eight hours, he didn't try to pretend he wasn't in love, didn't work on obscuring his emotions or locking her out of the secret areas of his heart.

And for once, she had responded in kind. She told him she loved him. She apologized for everything. She asked him for his forgiveness and promised that she was going to be true to him. She had her fun, and she was ready to settle down. Dominic, ready to pass his bar exam and begin the rest of his life on his own terms, saw no other choice but to propose.

"I asked her to marry me that weekend. We both knew it would be a long time before we tied the knot, but I wanted to stake my claim before she changed her mind again."

"Were you exclusive after that? Or did you both still...play the field?"

"No, we weren't monogamous. She was working with a fashion photographer at the time, and her job had her traveling all over the world for weeks at a time. She still had her fun and I still went to the BDSM clubs."

They were both collared though—she with a ring around her finger and he with the proverbial chain around his neck. He thought keeping her tied to his side would make him happy. He thought as long as he knew that her heart belonged to him, he could handle it if somebody else had her body. Perhaps most foolishly of all, he thought his heart was safe with her, and once they belonged to each other, everything would be easy.

They would be happy.

But he was no happier when she belonged to him than when she wouldn't commit to him. Other people still held very little interest in him, but the fascination he had for her diminished more and more over the years. Until he stayed because they were comfortable. Because she was a very good partner for him, professionally, and because he was good for her, too. Even with the way she acted out and attacked Sonya, Dominic didn't believe she still harbored sentimental feelings for him.

If she *ever* had sentimental feelings for him. It was literally impossible for him to say, one way or the other.

"After I had the agency established and things were looking good for me, we started talking about setting a date. It was the most serious that conversation ever got. But before anything could be fully settled, I saw you." Far too young for him. Far too good for him. Far too beautiful and vivacious and he knew even then that he should stay out of her way.

"When did you see me? When was that?"

"The first time I set eyes on you when you came into the office. Right after I hired your father."

Sonya's cheeks turned pink. "I was seventeen."

"Yeah. So I did everything I could to stop myself from thinking about you. And sometimes it worked. But mostly...so I knew I had to stay away from you. That's why I made a strict policy about no outsiders visiting the office. Everybody thought I was a real asshole but...well, I am, so that's okay."

"If you wanted to avoid me, why did you let me have the internship?" She lifted her head. "And why...at the club...?"

"Because I can only go the route of self-denial for so long. I didn't want to avoid you anymore. The club...was a test. I thought I had more self-control. I thought you would definitely say no. But I didn't, and you didn't say no." Dominic rattled his cuffs. "You can let me go. I'm not going to make a break for it."

"Not quite yet. How do I know that this woman who's had a hold over you you're entire adult life isn't going to bust in again?"

"Because you're the one I want."

"And she was the woman willing to fake a pregnancy to keep you! I mean, you've been involved with her one way or the other for twenty years, Dominic. And I'm just..."

"You're just what?"

"I'm barely an adult. What if you want something more? What if *I* want something more? I don't want you trying to put it all on me...what happens if I disappoint you?"

"Because for the first time in my life, I can see things

clearly. You love me, Sonya. And I love you. Whatev-er...whatever I feel about Fiona, it stopped being loved a long time ago."

"But I don't want to settle down."

"I'm not asking you to marry me. At least, not right now."

"I don't know how I feel about you going to BDSM clubs."

"I don't need to go if it makes you uncomfortable. I'm willing to compromise, Sonya. I'm willing to do whatever you need me to do."

Sonya looked up at him with luminous, glistening eyes. Without taking her gaze from his face, she released the catch on the cuffs, freeing his wrists and allowing him to drop his arms. He immediately engulfed her in a strong hug, holding her close despite the ache of exhaustion and tension in his muscles. She burrowed in closer, wrapping her arms around his torso and taking deep breaths as they settled together, their bodies fitting every nook and curve.

There was more to say. He knew she must have more questions. He waited, caught up in the rhythm of her breath, watching for dawn's light to break across the ceiling. He had no idea what time it was, but he knew it was still dark outside. Knew that everything could change by the light of day and he could still discover that he ruined every-thing, that he blew it with her and destroyed his shot at happiness. But at least the toxic relationship with Fiona had finally been forced to its bitter end, and if that's all that came out of his time with Sonya, he'd still have to count himself a fortunate man.

"You won't regret it," Dominic finally whispered, unable to stop himself from arguing his case. "And I'll spend the rest of my life proving it to you."

"You should take me out on a date."

"I can do that."

"And I want to go to a concert where I'm not the after-party."

Dominic grimaced slightly. No amount of explanation or apology will ever be enough to rectify that mistake.

"I'll take you to any concert you want. Wherever you want."

"And I want to know when I make you happy."

"You always make me happy. But I'm going to make sure that you know it, and everything else, from now on." He had been a rather poor Dom for her, giving her so much of what she needed, but never giving her all of it. Now he would. He'd give her everything she needed, everything she wanted.

"Kiss me."

"With pleasure, madam." He buried his hand in her hair and gripped the long tresses, holding her in place as he claimed her mouth with all the force of passion and desire that he hid from her before. Now there were no barriers between them. He wanted her to know how he burned for her, wanted to be honest and vulnerable in every way he could. She moaned into the kiss, responding in kind, giving back everything that she took from him. They sank down deeper and deeper into the mattress, lost in each other.

They were still kissing when the first ray of morning light touched through the window. Dominic wasn't in any hurry to do anything else, reacquainting himself with her mouth with slow, leisurely strokes of his tongue. She nestled down in his arms, her fingertips traveling up and down his chest, along his neck and over his jaw, through his hair, and along the line of his ear. He was almost painfully aware of every place she touched him, chills erupting over his skin from every point, every second of contact.

They were still kissing when he turned her onto her back, pressing her to the mattress with his weight, his thick cock nudging her thigh. Her legs fell open for him in the best, sweetest invitation he'd ever received, her knees bending to wrap around his hips.

With a sigh and a moan exchanged between their lips, he slid into her. Her body was ready, her flesh more than inviting, and her back arching off the bed to take him deep inside. Once he was fully inside her, he moved with slow strokes, shallow thrusts of his hips that kept him buried inside her perfect heat. Their tongues twined, and every groan and grunt, every shocked sound of pleasure, echoed from her to him and back again. His hand went to her hip, his thumb sliding along the curve to her thigh. Her skin was soft, perfect, and her muscles twitched at his touch, jumping at the slightest caress.

He followed the natural lines of her body until he pushed his thumb past her swollen pussy lips. Her clit was hard, throbbing every time he thrust inside of her, and her soft moans turned into a shocked shout when he pressed down on the twitching flesh. It was like hitting a switch, sending her body into the turbo-charged mode, her hips and her thighs and the great machine of her lovely body kicking up to the next gear.

Dominic lifted his head to watch her, eager to catch every flicker of pleasure, every change of expression as her breathing quickened and her pulse jumped at the base of her throat. Her hair was half out of the band she used to secure it, and he pulled it away completely, allowing the long tresses to frame her face and shoulders like a wild halo. She looked like an angel but she felt like a wildcat where she clawed at his back, her nails digging deep into his flesh. But the deeper they dug, the harder he pushed back, every sensation snowballing onto the next one.

She raked her fingers over his shoulder and clutched either side of his head, driving his mouth back down to hers. She tasted like all he ever needed, and Dominic wanted nothing more than to spill himself inside of her, empty himself into her until she was filled up with everything he was, and he could take a moment to rest, having given himself completely.

He massaged her clit with hard circles, pressing firmly on her flesh and guiding his thumb in a slow circle around the head and over the tip. She jerked each time he brushed over the sensitive hood, body clenching around him so tight that he thought she might break him right in two. He moved with her. They moved as one, and the feel of her was too much. Their dance was perfect, with a harmony of give-and-take that he'd never experienced before. Not with her. Not with anybody. This was the realization of all the potential between them, the moment when what he *believed* could be possible actually became a reality.

His reality.

"I'm so close," Sonya whimpered, more of a warning than a quandary.

"Me too, baby, me too. Come for me please, sweetheart, I need to feel it." Not an understatement. Perhaps the most truthful sentence he'd ever uttered. He *did* need to feel it. Feel her. Feel the two of them. Feel a connection that didn't frighten him—experience a moment that didn't have to stop when it was over. "Sonya, baby, let me feel you. Come right now for me."

Her body clenched around him and then on the next breath, she was breaking apart. And he was shattering into a million pieces around her. They clung to each other, slick with sweat, shaking and shivering and still rolling their hips. Rising and falling with each other, keeping the motion going until Dominic felt her building towards a second crest of pleasure. He pushed her, his mouth on her neck at the sensitive spot beneath her ear, his thumb grinding down on her clit.

"I'm so....oh *god.*" Her hips ratcheted up, moving hard and faster against him until she was fucking herself on his cock, and he was only following her lead. Even though he did come, his dick was still hard and he felt dozens of miniature explosions, like tiny fireworks, all up and down his spine. She clenched once again, her flesh so hot, her blood rushing so close to the surface that she was pink and flushed all over, and then her whole body unfurled, like a ripe blossom in the heat of summer.

Another explosion went off beneath his skin, but this one was much bigger—overwhelming and impossible. His cock jerked deep inside of her, though he had nothing left, and his whole body shook with the force of the pleasure, feeling the vibrations all the way down to his bones.

They collapsed together, their limbs still wrapped around each other's body, his half-soft cock still buried inside of her. They didn't speak. They didn't have anything left to say. They fell asleep like that, their mouths so close that they shared each breath.

CHAPTER 12

I NEED YOU

SONYA LISTENED to the steady ticking of the massive, oak grandfather clock, marking the passage of each second. Her heartbeat along with it, a steady, regular sound. She wasn't nervous. Her fingers tingled a little, and she stretched and wiggled them, trying to get the blood to flow back to the tips. The silk tie Dominic used as a blindfold was soft on her nose, tied securely so it wouldn't slip. It didn't allow a single speck of light, and she couldn't tell if she was sitting in the dark. Couldn't even tell if she was alone, or if Dominic was prowling through the room, circling the bed and watching her wait for him. The cuffs securing her to the bed were lined with fur, but they were tight, barely allowing her any room to move or twist her hands. Her ankles were similarly bound, holding her spread eagle across their massive mattress.

She knew Dominic could return at any time. It might be only a few seconds, or it might be another two hours. She was comfortable, though, and more than prepared to wait him out. She knew the waiting would be worth it. It always was.

In the three years since she moved in with him, she'd learned a great many lessons in the matter of patience. There was a pleasure in the wait. Pleasure in the anticipation of his touch. There was even pleasure in living with her own thoughts for a while. Some people went to the gym or do yoga to center themselves, clear their minds, and focus. But when the world got to be too much and she felt overwhelmed, confused, and tired, she went to Dominic. And Dominic always knew what his girl needed. Lying there in the center of their bed, the thick pillows beneath her back, the silk sheets wrapping around her legs, touching her like a lover, and nothing but the sound of their antique clock, she felt quiet. She felt peaceful.

She used to try to imagine what he would do to her. She tried to anticipate him, tried to rush to every new second and sensation, but he always kept better control of the situation. Now she relaxed. She let each moment flow over her, pain sliding into pleasure before she had the chance to catch her breath. She wasn't even sure if he was currently in the house. He might have slipped out the back door, or maybe he was making dinner downstairs. He might be on the computer or on his phone. But no matter what he was doing, she knew that he hadn't forgotten about her.

Sonya took a deep breath, feeling the air fill her lungs, holding it there for several beats of her heart, and then exhaled. Work had been exhausting that day and she had deadlines looming over her head. The next two months were completely booked, and this might be the last night she had for Dominic for a very long time. That thought made her sad. She loved her job as a paralegal, and she was nearly finished with her law degree, but sometimes she just wished she could hang everything up and spend her life in Dominic's bed.

The thing was...she could do that very thing. If she wanted to. He would be more than happy to support her, and down-right *thrilled* to come home to her waiting body every night. And there were some days that she gave it some serious thought. But ultimately, she liked that she was her own person, with her own life. Independent and autonomous, she knew she didn't need Dominic. She wasn't reliant on him and he wasn't holding her leash with a tight grip, keeping her at his side no matter what. Every night she chose to go home to him. She chose to submit to his desire and be chained to his bed.

That feeling was almost as good—or maybe even better—than the sensations he evoked with his touch and his oh-so-clever mind.

She knew the sound of his step, whether he was walking on plush carpet or hardwood floor. He used to be quite successful at sneaking up on her when he had her blind-folded, but now she could sense him. She heard him now, his light tread coming up the stairs. She felt herself tensing a little, her heart automatically speeding up, her pulse thundering at her throat. She swallowed down the excitement, tried to even out her breathing, but she was nearly trembling by the time he opened the door.

Dominic didn't speak. Sonya didn't greet him. The silence wrapped around the two of them, and even though she tried to be Zen about everything, she was waiting for his touch. Every inch of her wanted to feel his slightly callused fingertips. Every inch of her missed him when his body wasn't in contact with hers.

The bed dipped down under his weight, and she turned her head to the right, lips parted slightly for his kiss. He didn't disappoint. Sometimes, when he wanted to be kind, he didn't shave, allowing his stubble to grow out just enough to be rough against her lips. He started the kiss lightly, but Sonya was a little too hungry, a little too greedy, to allow it to remain so gentle. She returned the caress with passion, her lips burning for more. She broke away from the kiss to skim her lips over his jaw and chin and cheek, tongue flicking out occasionally before she returned to his waiting mouth.

Their tongue danced together, an intricate interplay they both knew well. Desire burned through her stomach while happiness pushed her heart to her throat. If her hands were free, she would have buried her fingers in his hair, would have smashed him even closer so she could devour him. His breath had a tinge of whiskey, and the taste of the alcohol made her tongue tingle, but it was him that warmed her through, thawing away the icy stress of the day.

. . .

The kiss went on and on. She was in no hurry to break it. Sometimes it still felt so amazing, so *weird*, to be kissing him like this. She could kiss him whenever she wanted. She could claim his mouth and sear her desire into his flesh at any point, any minute of the day she chose to, and it still felt so new. So raw. Fortunately, he was as thorough as she was, in no hurry to break the connection they've both longed for all day.

He didn't want her to quit her job just to be home all day. He wanted her to come back to his office and work, but Sonya knew no work would be done. They would just spend the entire day in his office fucking, and while she liked the idea in theory, she knew they needed to be productive people. Besides, when they were finally alone together, it was even better after all the hours they were apart. Every minute was used to make up for the lost time and not a second was wasted between them.

When they finally broke apart, she was flushed and out of breath. He nuzzled against her cheek and her neck, a sweet gesture, his warm breath fanning over her skin. She tilted her head back, allowing him room to lick at her throat, his tongue lingering over her beating pulse. She swallowed, trying to keep the butterflies in her chest under control. The scent of his aftershave surrounded her head, but she sensed his real scent beneath it and tasted the salt of his skin on her lips. His lips nibbled at the base of her throat, his teeth scraping across her thin skin. She caught her breath and arched into him, silently encouraging him to do more than scrape over her skin.

He didn't give her what she wanted, of course. His tongue danced patterns over her throbbing flesh, expertly winding her up, making her twitch and writhe against the mattress. She held back her whimpers, not wanting to break so early in the evening, but every ounce of her wanted to beg him to please, *please*, bite down. Not that she needed words. He knew what she wanted. He always knew. He understood every desire long before she ever thought to give them a voice.

Finally, she felt the sharp points of his teeth. Delicately at first. No more than a hint of pressure. Her pulse still jumped, her head falling back even further. When he clenched his jaw, biting down hard enough to hurt, she cried out, her cuffs rattling as she reflexively tried to reach for him. She wanted to hold his head and press him closer. Her clit throbbed, and though he wasn't touching her below her neck, she felt like his hands were roving all over her body, like his fingers were buried between her wet folds.

He released her, repositioned his mouth higher up her neck, and bit down with the same pressure. He did that again and again, covering her neck and shoulder in love bites, not using enough force to leave a mark, but she still tingled from the pressure, still moaned in appreciation and need. No matter how much he gave her, it wasn't enough. And if he kept it up, she would come before he even let his fingers drift down her body.

. . .

"You're very tense," he said, mouth moving against her skin. "Hard day?"

"Mmmhmm."

He bit a path across her shoulder. His hair tickled against her skin as he began his journey lower. Her nipples hardened into stiff points before he even got to the swell of her breasts, and his tongue laved over them, following the curve but never reaching the rosy skin that begged for his attention. She shifted a little, arching her back, holding her breath until his soft skin and rough bristle finally came in contact with her sensitive nipples. Again, she could barely hold back her pleas for more. She couldn't stop the soft whimper, though, when the tip of his tongue skimmed over the tip of her pebbly flesh.

"I have something for you." He breathed hot air across her trembling flesh.

"I know you do."

He chuckled. "Something else. A special treat. Do you want it first?"

"What is it?"

. . .

"It's a surprise."

"Then how am I supposed to know if I want it?"

"Are you hungry?"

Just as he asked that, her stomach clenched and growled, and she remembered she skipped both breakfast and lunch that day. A fact she had completely forgotten in the interest of getting her other appetite satisfied, but now that he mentioned it, the hunger for food was far more pressing than the hunger for his touch.

He heard the growling in her stomach and chuckled. "That's what I thought. I know you skipped your breakfast this morning, you naughty girl."

"And lunch too," she admitted.

"You can't be doing that."

"You skip meals."

"I'm a bad influence. Do as I say, not as I do. Now, having said that..." He straightened, and she instantly regretted the lack of contact. She could deal with her hunger as long as he was touching her, but now she felt hollow inside and bereft. She couldn't help her small moan of impatience—a sound that might earn her a punishment any other day, but he seemed to be in a good mood, and all he did was chuckle again. *He's in a very good mood. There must be good news.*

"Open up."

She obeyed, not sure what to expect. Dominic was a pretty accomplished chef—somewhere along the way of his life he had taken to cooking like a duck to water. She expected a refined concoction with layers of flavor—she definitely got layers of flavor but she would never think to characterize an ice cream sundae as *refined.* But this one was more than amazing. Silky sweet vanilla bean ice cream melted against her tongue, caught between the heat of her mouth and the heat of the rich, warm fudge sauce. Smashed peanuts and Oreo cookies added a bit of crunch, a good contrast to the soft banana that completed her small bite.

Sonya swallowed it down and opened her mouth for more, her sweet tooth delighted by the surprise.

"I take it you like that."

She nodded eagerly. She liked the second, slightly larger bite, even more, letting the dessert linger in her mouth for a few moments before swallowing it down. The third bite was immediately followed by the hot press of Dominic's mouth. She automatically parted her lips, and when she did, his tongue swooped in and stole some of the ice cream and fudge away. She tried to get it back, their tongues dueling playfully until he leaned back. When he returned, the ice cream was melting on his tongue, and it was her turn to swoop in and scoop it away, getting the taste of him mingled with the sweet treat.

He was apparently in a playful mood. He drizzled the cold ice cream over her chest, following it up with the contrast of hot fudge. She wiggled as the melting dessert dripped over her nipple and down the side of her breasts, bucking with pleasure when he chased each drop with his eager lips. He licked the sticky mess away until she was clean again, and then repeated the process, lower and lower, over her stomach, over her hips, over her thighs. She splayed her legs as far as she could, gasping for breath when the warm fudge hit her swollen folds. His tongue felt all the hotter as he licked her flesh clean before delicately pulling her skin apart, allowing him access to her swollen clit.

He paused for a moment, and when she felt his tongue again, it was cold from another bite of ice cream. She yelped, her hips bucking, the cold sensation disappearing after only a few seconds against her overheated flesh. Her blood thrummed through her body, rushing south as he wiggled his tongue over her. Her clit became more swollen, and he pressed his mouth against her pussy, sucking the hard flesh between his teeth. A single finger slipped down her body, into her slick hole, filling her passage. That wasn't enough for her, and he knew it. But she had to be patient. Had to cling to her patience in the face of the growing fires, pleasure rushing through her from head to toe.

Sonya was so wet for more that it was easy for him to add a second finger as he attacked her with his mouth. Her thighs trembled. He worked in a third finger. The more he stretched her open, the more she became aware that his fingers were not going to be enough. She felt completely hollow, *needing* to be filled by him, her frustration mounting by the second as she became more and more aware of her need. He could work on her pussy with his mouth and fingers all night, and the orgasm would elude her. Leaving her all the more frustrated. She needed *him*. Nothing else mattered, ultimately. Nobody else mattered.

The past three years hadn't always been easy. He was still set in his ways, used to being completely independent. And Fiona wasn't exactly accustomed to being without him. She still surfaced every once in a while, thinking maybe he'd grown tired of his "little tart" and had "come to his senses." He always shut her out completely, but Sonya knew that wouldn't stop her from trying again and again. Possibly for the rest of her life. Sometimes insecurity clutched her. Sometimes she doubted that she could keep a man like Dominic satisfied and happy and in the back of her mind, she feared that he would find another hot, young number. A girl just like her, who was all wide-eyed innocence. Sometimes she worried about herself. She had so little experience in the world, and what if somebody else came along who set her heart racing and her blood on fire? What if Dominic wasn't the only one for her and she felt the pull of temptation?

But when they were together like this, her fears were so insignificant. So meaningless. When they were together like this, she knew she had nothing to fear at all. He felt every ounce of desire that coursed through her, knew the same frustration and knew the same disappointment when the world and obligations kept them apart. She knew he did because when they finally came together, when he finally pushed inside of her, like he was coming home, there was such a sense of shared relief.

She needed that now, and she finally gave voice to the clawing desire.

"Please, Dom...Please fuck me. I need to feel you inside of me."

"It's not time for that yet."

Sonya didn't need an argument. She didn't want his timetable. "*Please*. I need you. All day. I've needed you. I've needed this."

. . .

Dominic spoke the language of need. If nothing else, he understood the words, the tones, the nuances of pure *need*. And though he didn't usually let her dictate the terms of their coupling, he rarely denied her requests. He disappeared from her for a moment, but when he returned, she felt the warmth of his skin, the scratching texture of the hair on his legs and his chest as he moved to cover her body. She was open and slick for him and the tip of his cock nudged against her lips and then slipped inside with an easy thrust. She rose up to meet him, her muscles pulling tight as she clenched around his hot, thick shaft.

"Oh...sweetheart..."

He ripped the blindfold from her eyes and smashed their mouths together. Even without the blindfold, she kept her eyes tightly closed, trying to process the sensations of his cock, his tongue, his solid chest, his breath, his whiskers. He put his hands under her ass, cupping her flesh and lifting her to meet each thrust. She rose with him, pushing herself into each thrust, taking him as deep as she possibly could.

He knew how to play her body like a fine instrument. She used to think that reaching orgasm was the only goal. Now he could push her to her peak of pleasure within moment, knowing the right angle, the right rhythm to send her into the stratosphere. And once he got there, he maintained it, setting off a series of small explosions that grew larger and larger until she was overwhelmed, bombarded by constant, heated pleasure. The rest of the world fell away. The way it always been when she was in his arms. All that mattered was the two of them, and all she heard was his ragged breathing and the sound of the clock, ticking off their seconds together, sending them into their bright future, hand in hand

ABOUT THE AUTHOR

Heather Stolts is an emerging erotica author of many erotica kinks and sub-genres. Be sure to check out other books and leave a review if this story got you hot!

Visit my blog at Heather Stolts Blog

Join my newsletter for exclusive previews Heather Stolts Newsletter

Sign up for Free Stories from Xplicit Press Authors

Xplicit Press Author Updates

Like Xplicit Press on Facebook

Follow Xplicit Press on Twitter

Readers: I want to expand a few of the stories to see where the characters can be explored further. If there are any of the stories that you would like to read more about again, I'd love to hear from you!

Keep In Touch
Heather Stolts
info@heatherstolts.com